Aliens of the Heart

Conversation Pieces

A Small Paperback Series from Aqueduct Press

Subscriptions available: www.aqueductpress.com

1. The Grand Conversation
   Essays by L. Timmel Duchamp
2. With Her Body
   Short Fiction by Nicola Griffith
3. Changeling
   A Novella by Nancy Jane Moore
4. Counting on Wildflowers
   An Entanglement by Kim Antieau
5. The Traveling Tide
   Short Fiction by Rosaleen Love
6. The Adventures of the Faithful Counselor
   A Narrative Poem by Anne Sheldon
7. Ordinary People
   A Collection by Eleanor Arnason
8. Writing the Other
   A Practical Approach
   by Nisi Shawl & Cynthia Ward
9. Alien Bootlegger
   A Novella by Rebecca Ore
10. The Red Rose Rages (Bleeding)
    A Short Novel by L. Timmel Duchamp
11. Talking Back: Epistolary Fantasies
    edited by L. Timmel Duchamp
12. Absolute Uncertainty
    Short Fiction by Lucy Sussex

13. Candle in a Bottle
    A Novella by Carolyn Ives Gilman

14. Knots
    Short Fiction by Wendy Walker

15. Naomi Mitchison: A Profile of Her Life and Work
    A Monograph by Lesley A. Hall

16. We, Robots
    A Novella by Sue Lange

17. Making Love in Madrid
    A Novella by Kimberly Todd Wade

18. Of Love and Other Monsters
    A Novella by Vandana Singh

19. Aliens of the Heart
    Short Fiction by Carolyn Ives Gilman

20. Voices From Fairyland:
    The Fantastical Poems of Mary Coleridge, Charlotte Mew, and Sylvia Townsend Warner
    Edited and With Poems by Theodora Goss

21. My Death
    A Novella by Lisa Tuttle

22. De Secretis Mulierum
    A Novella by L. Timmel Duchamp

23. Distances
    A Novella by Vandana Singh

24. Three Observations and a Dialogue:
    Round and About SF
    Essays by Sylvia Kelso and a correspondence with Lois McMaster Bujold

25. The Buonarotti Quartet
    Short Fiction by Gwyneth Jones

26. Slightly Behind and to the Left
    Four Stories & Three Drabbles by Claire Light

27. Through the Drowsy Dark
    Short Fiction and Poetry
    by Rachel Swirsky

28. Shotgun Lullabies
    Stories and Poems by Sheree Renée Thomas

29. A Brood of Foxes
    A Novella by Kristin Livdahl

30. The Bone Spindle
    Poems and Short Fiction by Anne Sheldon

31. The Last Letter
    A Novella by Fiona Lehn

32. We Wuz Pushed
    On Joanna Russ and Radical Truth-Telling
    by Brit Mandelo

33. The Receptionist and Other Tales
    Poems by Lesley Wheeler

34. Birds and Birthdays
    Stories by Christopher Barzak

35. The Queen, the Cambion, and Seven Others
    Stories by Richard Bowes

36. Spring in Geneva
    A Novella by Sylvia Kelso

37. The XY Conspiracy
    A Novella by Lori Selke

38. Numa
    An Epic Poem
    by Katrinka Moore

39. Myths, Metaphors, and Science Fiction:
    Ancient Roots of the Literature of the Future
    Essays by Sheila Finch

40. NoFood
    Short Fiction by Sarah Tolmie

41. The Haunted Girl
    Poetry and Short Stories by Lisa M. Bradley

41. The Haunted Girl
    Poetry and Short Stories by Lisa M. Bradley

42. Three Songs for Roxy
    A Novella by Caren Gussoff

43. Ghost Signs
    Poems and a Short Story by Sonya Taaffe

44. The Prince of the Aquamarines & The Invisible Prince: Two Fairy Tales
    by Louise Cavelier Levesque

45. Back, Belly, and Side: True Lies and False Tales
    by Celeste Rita Baker

46. A Day in Deep Freeze
    A Novella by Lisa Shapter

47. A Field Guide to the Spirits
    Poems by Jean LeBlanc

48. Marginalia to Stone Bird
    Poems by Rose Lemberg

49. Unpronounceable
    A Novella by Susan diRende

50. Sleeping Under the Tree of Life
    Poetry and Short Fiction by Sheree Renée Thomas

51. Other Places
    Short Fiction by Karen Heuler

52. Monteverde: Memoirs of an Interstellar Linguist
    A Novella by Lola Robles,
    translated by Lawrence Schimel

53. The Adventure of the Incognita Countess
    A Novella by Cynthia Ward

54. Boundaries, Border Crossings, and Reinventing the Future
    Essays and Short Fiction by Beth Plutchak

55. Liberating the Astronauts
    Poems by Christina Rau

56. In Search of Lost Time
    A Novella by Karen Heuler

About the Aqueduct Press Conversation Pieces Series

The feminist engaged with sf is passionately interested in challenging the way things are, passionately determined to understand how everything works. It is my constant sense of our feminist-sf present as a grand conversation that enables me to trace its existence into the past and from there see its trajectory extending into our future. A genealogy for feminist sf would not constitute a chart depicting direct lineages but would offer us an ever-shifting, fluid mosaic, the individual tiles of which we will probably only ever partially access. What could be more in the spirit of feminist sf than to conceptualize a genealogy that explicitly manifests our own communities across not only space but also time?

Aqueduct's small paperback series, Conversation Pieces, aims to both document and facilitate the "grand conversation." The Conversation Pieces series presents a wide variety of texts, including short fiction (which may not always be sf and may not necessarily even be feminist), essays, speeches, manifestoes, poetry, interviews, correspondence, and group discussions. Many of the texts are reprinted material, but some are new. The grand conversation reaches at least as far back as Mary Shelley and extends, in our speculations and visions, into the continually-created future. In Jonathan Goldberg's words, "To look forward to the history that will be, one must look at and retell the history that has been told." And that is what Conversation Pieces is all about.

L. Timmel Duchamp

Jonathan Goldberg, "The History That Will Be" in Louise Fradenburg and Carla Freccero, eds., *Premodern Sexualities* (New York and London: Routledge, 1996)

Conversation Pieces
Volume 19

Aliens of the Heart

Short Fiction

by

Carolyn Ives Gilman

Published by Aqueduct Press
PO Box 95787
Seattle, WA 98145-2787
www.aqueductpress.com

 First Edition, October 2007

ISBN: 978-1-933500-17-1

Book Design by Kathryn Wilham
Original Block Print of Mary Shelley by Justin Kempton:
www.writersmugs.com

Cover illustration by Kathryn Wilham

Cover photo of Pleiades Star Cluster
NASA Hubble Telescope Images, STScI-2004-20
http://hubble.nasa.gov/image-gallery/astronomy-images.html
Credit: NASA, ESA, and AURA/Caltech

For Rhoda, from her biggest fan

Table of Contents

Lost Road

It was a dry year. Come June, the corn that should have been knee-high was stunted and papery in the fields; the pasture grass rustled, stiff as broom straw, in the constant wind. The topsoil had turned powdery, and you could see it blowing off the fields in clouds, making the sunsets red.

To Betty Lindstrom it seemed like her whole world was drying up and blowing away. She and Wayne had had to lease out the last 40 acres that spring to a man from the next county who was farming nearly all the land in their township. He'd taken out the fences and cut down the beech-tree windbreaks Betty's father had planted in the '30s, and now plowed fields came right up to the edge of the farmhouse yard on every side.

After supper one evening Betty took Chipper and walked out to the endless cornfield where her grandfather's original farmstead had been. She stood with the wind blowing strands of gray hair in her eyes, trying to trace the outline of the foundations. But they had been scraped away, planted over. Just like Wayne had been scraped away by the stroke, his wit and cheer dried up, powdered, and scoured in the wind.

Betty drove Wayne into the town of Lost Road every week, inching along in their 1978 Volare with Chipper in the back seat. She didn't like driving. Wayne had always done the driving before the stroke. Whenever she sat down behind the wheel with him to her right, it made her aware that the man she had married was gone and a stranger now shared her life. The county road blurred in front of her, a straight line meeting the horizon in a T. Every now and then another car would come along, and she would veer over onto the shoulder 'till it was safely by.

Their car was the only thing moving on the main street of Lost Road. The buildings were weathered, colorless, and spaced too far apart. A block off the main street the derelict shells of old grain elevators stood along what had once been a Soo Line feeder track. Around them the prairie had begun to reseed itself.

The gas station stood under an old Pure sign no one had ever bothered to take down. Its garage door was always open, revealing a cluttered, grease-stained interior. Betty had never been inside the garage; that was a man's world. She had been in the office a few times and remembered faded packs of gum under a glass counter frosted by a half-century of quarters passing over it. No one was around, so they helped themselves from the single pump, filling the car and the two five-gallon cans in the trunk for the generator. Wayne shuffled into the office, his overalls hanging loose on his stick-thin body, his visored cap saying CENEX. Dan Erickson would soon show up. They'd talk field hands and field goals, forward passes and tillage passes. Wayne would say, in that old-man way he had now, how hard farming used to be and how glad he was to be out of it. And he would fool no one.

Betty drove on down to the corner store. Inside, the dusty windows cast a tired light on half-empty racks of drugstore sundries. Betty picked up some toilet paper, bread, bananas, and milk.

"How you getting through this dry weather?" Dot Meyers said when Betty brought her purchases to the counter.

"Oh, we're okay," Betty said.

"Didn't see you at church last Sunday. We get kind of worried about you, you know, out there all alone in that farmhouse."

"We're doing just fine," Betty said. It was none of Dot's business anyhow. Wayne had always teased Betty about being a deadpan Swede who never let any troubles show. She probably was, and too late to change now.

"We had a big meeting about our Lost Road Days festival," Dot said, taking a hand-printed sheet and sticking it in Betty's grocery bag. "We're looking for people to make things for the bake sale."

Dot was always trying to organize things.

"I'll think about it," Betty said.

As she carried her bag out to the car where Chipper waited, Betty looked over Dot's flyer. On the back it had a typed paragraph about the history of the town.

Lost Road was founded in the 1870s, when New York speculator Jeremiah Parker surveyed a road over his land holdings between the Yellow Medicine and Big Sioux rivers. Returning east, he published a map showing the road studded with towns. He induced several hundred settlers to buy land and move west.

But when they arrived they found none of the promised road, traffic, or towns. The hardy pioneers among them who survived the first winter called the fiasco "Parker's Lost Road."

∞

As she started the car, Betty had a strange, reckless idea. What if she just turned east instead of west and drove off out of town? What if she just left Wayne at the gas station and didn't come back? But deep down she knew she didn't really want to get away from Wayne. He was a part of her, like arthritis. No point complaining.

They left town about 4:20, driving west. The sun glared into the windshield from a cloudless sky. Red-winged blackbirds flew up from the unmowed ditches as the car passed. Down the roadside, telephone poles marched in an endless procession. Every few miles they passed the remains of old driveways that used to lead to farmhouses. Every year the land was getting emptier. They said farming was a business now, not a way of life.

"We've got to go back," Wayne said suddenly.

"Why?"

"We didn't get the mail."

"Yes, I did. It's in the bag. Your magazine came."

He didn't turn to get it. Their daughter Alice had sent him the subscription, but he never read it.

"Alice hasn't called for months," Wayne said.

"She called just last Saturday," Betty said.

"How come you didn't tell me?"

"I did. You talked to her. You just don't remember."

Alice was off in the city having a life filled with events. A trip to Hawaii, a job reassignment, her daughter competing in a state tennis tournament. Betty couldn't remember events like that ever happening to her. Her life was more like the paper than the writing—the background you had to have in order to see the ink.

Betty realized she had been driving automatically, not seeing where she was going. "Did I miss the turnoff?" she asked. But Wayne just shrugged. Betty slowed down. She kept expecting to see their house ahead. Though she couldn't place just where they were, she knew they were close.

In all the landscape the only thing moving was a combine far away on the horizon, big as a factory on wheels. Betty's thoughts strayed back to those settlers who'd followed Jeremiah Parker's map out here, imagining towns and communities and finding only prairie and wind. She didn't think they were heroic at all. They'd been duped into believing legends. She could almost feel their bitterness and longing around her, as if their dust was in the air.

At last Betty decided she'd gone too far, and when they came to a dirt township road she turned around.

After half an hour the road ahead still looked exactly the same. Betty was puzzled; she had driven far enough to be all the way back in Lost Road by now. She pulled to the shoulder and stopped.

"What's the problem?" Wayne asked.

"Do you know where we are?" Betty said.

"I thought we were going home."

Betty didn't want to say she couldn't find their house. She'd been driving this stretch all her life. "I guess it's a little farther on," she said, and started up again.

Everything looked familiar, just like deja vu. Before long she had convinced herself she was on Highway 35, driving parallel to the county road. No wonder she couldn't find their house. When she came to a township road she turned south.

"I've got to pee," Wayne said plaintively.

"Why didn't you go at the station?"

"I didn't have to then. We've been driving a long time."

When he had to go, he had to go. Betty pulled over. Wayne got out and shambled over to the grassy ditch. Betty got up to let the dog out, shoes crunching on gravel. Grasshoppers buzzed in the heat.

When she looked over to see if Wayne was done, he was staring fixedly out across the ditch. "What're those?" he said, pointing.

The low hill was dotted with uniform rows of gray cylinders lying on their sides. They were too big for oil drums, and they looked purposefully arranged, like manufactured artifacts. Betty squinted, searching for an explanation to quell her rising sense of the sinister.

Then she laughed. "Hay bales," she said. "They don't make them square any more, you know, Dad. They're all round like that these days."

But as she shooed Chipper back into the car, she felt fear at her own confusion. Why had they looked so strange for a second? They ought to be so familiar.

They drove on. The telephone poles by the road were casting long cross-shadows over the grassy banks, and birds perched on the wires like silent notes of music. "This is the same road," Betty said. "The same road we were on before."

She speeded up, desperate to get somewhere, anywhere. She scanned the fields for the telltale groves of oak and elm, each with a clutch of white buildings nestled underneath. That was the landscape she recognized. But it wasn't here now. No warm, buttery light leaking out past gingham curtains, no dogs in the yard wagging a welcome, no noisy kitchens inviting them in. It was all just legends now.

The sun was on the horizon by the time she came to a deserted crossroad and stopped.

Wayne, who had fallen asleep, roused and looked around. "Where are we?" he asked.

"I don't know," Betty said.

"You mean we're lost?"

He took it very calmly. Matter-of-fact, as if this happened all the time. They sat together on the bumper of the car, eating bread and bananas and watching the sunset. Chipper nosed around in the roadside grass. Eventually he came up to beg, and Betty poured him some milk and gave him bread.

The wind had died down, and the only sound was the crickets. "I know where we are," Wayne said suddenly. "This is Brown's Corner."

Of course. Across the road was the spot where Brown's store had stood, and behind it the pasture where they used to show movies on a sheet strung between two phone poles. She could remember the grass parked full of Model Ts, and people from miles around sitting on plaid blankets. It had been a night just like this, with a wide-open sky above, when she and Wayne had shared an ice cream and she'd decided he was the one she wanted to spend her life with.

"I chased you for ten years, you know," she said.

"Yeah, I was Mr. Popularity back then. Remember how we used to go dancing? Glenn Miller. Now that was *music.*" He began humming. "Hey, I bet you still can dance."

"Not me," Betty said, smiling. He hadn't acted like this for ages.

He fell silent, and Betty gradually remembered that Brown's Corner was back in Blue Earth County where they'd grown up, not out here.

Wayne slept on the back seat that night. Betty lay awake in the front, listening to time pass.

∽

She was wakened by the roar of a semi. She sat up in a daze to catch sight of the back of the truck disappearing down the highway. It was broad daylight. She woke Wayne, and they breakfasted on bread and milk. The sight of the semi had put her in good spirits. She was embarrassed to think of her confusion the evening before. Now she knew they would soon find a town and be home before noon.

And in fact they had only been driving for half an hour when grain elevators appeared on the horizon to the south. As they drew closer, Betty could make out the white steeple of a church and the roofs of houses. She kept expecting the road to veer toward the town, but instead it continued on west, straight as a ruler. Betty looked with fading hope for a crossroad leading south. Somehow, she knew there would be none—and even if there were, it would not lead to the town.

She stopped the car and looked out across the fields. It was no more than a mile or two to walk, but Wayne could never make it, and she couldn't leave him alone in the hot car. She willed back the frustrated tears that filled her eyes. She wanted nothing more than to see a Safeway sign or a Rexall drug store. She wanted to call out across the fields, "Here I am!" But her voice was a thin, old-lady voice now. No one would hear her.

The road rolled by, familiar as ever. They crossed an Interstate, but there was no exit or entrance, and a tall chain-link fence kept them from the roadside. They stopped on the bridge and tried to signal cars to stop, but no one understood.

They drove on.

"Maybe we could signal an airplane," Wayne said as they sat resting by the roadside that afternoon.

Betty poured the last of the milk into Chipper's bowl, and he lapped it up thirstily. "You mean lay our clothes out on the ground in an SOS?" she asked.

"You want to take off your clothes?" he said. She looked at him in surprise; there was laughter in his eyes that hadn't been there for a year.

"Not me," she said.

"Then maybe we ought to just flash a mirror at them. You've got a mirror in your purse, don't you? You've got everything in there."

There was no mirror in her purse, so they decided to break the rear-view mirror off the windshield. They stood in the middle of the deserted road, trying to catch the sun in an SOS pattern. But all the planes they saw were jets so high they were just specks in the cloudless sky. "They'll never see," Betty said.

That evening they stopped at a place where a railroad embankment crossed the road. Betty and Wayne strolled arm-in-arm up to the tracks, Chipper at their heels. Field mice skittered across the cindery railroad bed, and the smell of old creosote rose from the sun-baked ties. Betty stood gazing at the tracks curving off into the west. She felt sure these must be the old Northern Pacific tracks that went out to the coast.

"My brother Lars went away to work on this railroad when I was a kid," she said to Wayne. She remembered standing just like this as a girl, when the tracks had been the golden road to Seattle and the Orient. Lars had brought her back a black enamel jewelry box with Chinese scenes painted on it in gold. She'd wanted then to follow the tracks off the farm, but never did it. And now the tracks didn't really gleam any more; in fact, they looked rusty and unused.

"I know what our problem is," she said suddenly. "We're on the lost road. It's got to be. Those old settlers imagined it so hard it just came to be. No wonder it doesn't connect to anything."

They drove aimlessly the next day. They put the extra gas into the tank, but even that gradually dwindled away. Betty felt tired and thirsty. She was sure there had to be some way off this imaginary road. When they turned on the radio the Marshall station came through just fine. They were so close.

As twilight fell, they spotted a homey light coming from curtained windows in a little grove far across the cornfields. It looked so warm and inviting Betty felt a surge of desperation. She jerked the wheel to the side, and the car jolted over the shoulder and through the ditch. Its wheels spun a moment, then it lurched into the field.

"Whoa! What are you doing?" Wayne said.

"I'm leaving the road. I'm going to drive right over the field. Maybe that's the answer."

The car bounced over the corn rows, its bumper breaking off brittle stalks. Wayne looked aghast at the damage she was doing to the field. They were almost at the top of a rise when the back wheel sank into a deep trap of powdery soil. Betty put the car in reverse and tried to back out, but the wheel spun deeper. They were stuck.

Betty laid her head down against the wheel. The mad drive through the field had taken the last of her energy. She couldn't cope any longer.

At last she said dully, "Well, that was pretty dumb."

"I don't know what there is left to do that's very smart," Wayne said. It was so like something the old Wayne would have said that tears came to her eyes. To hide them, she got out. She let the dog out of the back seat, then walked on to the top of the rise, hugging herself tight. When she got there she stood looking out over the broad, rolling landscape growing dark under the fading sky. There were no lights, no houses as far as the eye could see. So that window she'd seen had been another mirage, another disappointment. Well, she was used to that.

Chipper, sensing her distress, pressed against her leg. She heard the car door slam behind her, and Wayne's footsteps. He stopped a few feet away.

"Don't worry, Betty," he said. "It'll all be okay."

Her throat was aching. He stepped closer and spoke softly, a little joking. "Hey, don't worry, I'm still here. As long as we stick together, we got no problems we can't solve."

It was the old Wayne's voice. The tears she'd been holding back for months suddenly came, rain on parched earth. She turned and hugged him, hugged him tighter than she ever had. "Don't ever leave me again," she said, her face pressed tight against his shoulder. "I've been lonelier than I thought I could be."

"It's okay," he said, then just held her and patted her on the back. It took a long time for all the tears she hadn't cried to come out. At last he gave her a hug and took her hand. "It's okay," he said again.

"Yeah," she said, wiping her face. "I guess it is now."

They walked back down the hill and sat in the dirt with their backs against the car and their arms around each other. Chipper lay down with his head on Betty's ankle.

"Hey, I know what to do," Wayne said.

He got up and switched on the car radio. A sweet old Glenn Miller song was playing. He sat back down beside her.

"I suppose we should have kept on following the road, wherever it went," Betty said.

"Oh, I don't know," said Wayne. "I don't think there was any right or wrong thing to do. You just do your best."

Betty was gazing off toward the west. The horizon looked rumpled, like an unmade bed. "Wayne, look," she said.

"What?"

"Clouds. There's rain coming."

"So there is."

They sat there as night fell, watching the rain clouds sweep slowly toward them over the land.

Frost Painting

Soon after Galena Pittman's plane landed in Williston, North Dakota, she began to pick up nuggets of valuable information. To wit:

1. They really listen to Country Western music in the country west. Monotonous, whining hours of it, in fact.
2. Edible vegetables are as rare there as art critics.
3. Don't depend on public transportation if you want to get somewhere before dehydration sets in.

"I'll just catch a cab," she said to the woman at the ticket counter in the one-room Williston airport. The woman was dressed in the polyester pant suit all small-town females seemed required to wear, and she had that rural look of certainty that she knew how the land lay. Right now she was regarding Galena as if she were a six-year-old who needed life explained to her.

"The cab drivers will both be at home," she said.

"*Both*?" Galena said.

"It's suppertime," the ticket woman said, efficiently piling up papers.

She cast an eye over Galena, taking in the stylish bolo tie with the ceramic cactus pin, the wide-brimmed hat with the quail feather, the hand-painted cowboy boots. Her left eyebrow rose.

"How am I supposed to get to the motel, then?" Galena said. Outside, there was nothing in sight but range land. It was going to be a long walk.

At last the woman sighed. "I'll give you a lift."

Climbing into the woman's pickup, it occurred to Galena that the context had changed the message of her clothing since she had left Chicago that morning. Normally, she took pride in dressing with the kind of riskiness that said to onlookers, "This is a trained professional. Do not try this at home." But here the cultural referents were different.

"I suppose you think I'm intending to be satirical," she said as the truck thudded across cattle grates onto the highway, bouncing her off the seat. "Actually, I'm making a kind of reflexive commentary on the banalization of the Western motif in the mass market."

No reaction.

"It's a statement on Eastern use of Western symbols. I'm satirizing us, not you."

"You heading for the Windrow Mountains?" the woman said.

"Yes." Galena was surprised to be found out so quickly.

"I figured. You're the type."

The type? Galena would admit to being many things, but not a *type*.

"We've been getting a lot of you through here," the woman went on. "Arty types."

Kooks. Weirdos. Galena could almost hear the woman thinking the words. "I'm not going there to stay," she said. "Joining a hive-mind's not my thing. I'm not a Californian."

"Uh-huh," the woman said.

There was something like a siren that went off in Galena's mind at times like this. It was whooping, *wrong, wrong*. She had made a fool of herself again. It was like a career.

The next morning when Galena picked up the white rental Hyundai at the Chevrolet dealership, the boots and bolo were gone. Even so, the car dealer spotted her right away. Guessing where she was bound, he turned suddenly reluctant to rent her the car.

"Look, I'm just going there to see a friend," Galena said reasonably. "I'll be back Sunday."

"So you say."

"You want to see my plane ticket?"

"You all have plane tickets."

Exasperated, Galena said, "Have they ever heard of tolerance in this town?"

"It's easy for you East Coasters to be tolerant," the man said. "You don't have to live near them. I'll tell you this: if those weirdos ever decide to come out of the mountains, we're going to be ready for them. That is, if you liberals haven't taken away our guns by then, too."

Galena would have gladly gotten into a scrap with the man, but there was no time. She ended up leaving a signed credit-card slip with him to cover the cost of retrieving the car, if necessary.

Unfolding the map on her dashboard, she saw that south and west of Williston was nothing but blank space with anemic gray lines wandering through it. "Road condition unknown," the map said helpfully. "Hi ho Silver," Galena said to the Hyundai. Then she put on her sunglasses and prepared to cross the Great Plains in a Korean rattletrap.

"I hope you appreciate this, Thea," she said.

"Galena Pittman," a rival columnist had once written, "is aptly named for a poisonous mineral." The phrase had amused Galena's colleagues so annoyingly that she had adopted it, mentioning it so often and laughing so hard that everyone began to realize it stung her.

In fact, Galena had been stinging since she was born. Long ago she had realized she was the world's pincushion, a target for every petty mortification, every nettling slight the world could invent. She could chew her cuticles raw thinking of the condescensions she had to endure in a given day, the premeditated cruelties of cabmen and bureaucrats. The only defense was to attack earlier and more wittily, to wear a coat of banter thick enough to keep the pins away. It rarely worked.

Her mother had a favorite saying: "If you make a bed of nails for yourself, you'd better lie on it, and like it." Galena had spent a lifetime casting barbs at that slogan, trying to find ways to disprove it.

In college, she had wanted to be an artist; but she had soon learned that she couldn't bear to see others looking at her work, thinking thoughts she couldn't control. She had tried to explain herself so intrusively, and had annoyed so many people, that it finally dawned on her that the explaining was all she was really good at. So, unable to be criticized, she became a critic.

Galena had actually fallen in love with Thea Nodine's art several minutes before she fell in love with the artist herself. It had happened on a day when her landlord had decided to repair the plaster without any notice, and she had spent most of an hour calling everyone she knew to come help her move furniture, receiving only one recorded message after another. At last, where friendship failed, money had to take over. The people at Hank's Hauling had been only too happy to help, once they had taken her Visa number hostage. By evening her apartment was in chaos, and Galena was in a state of advanced disappointment with the world. She wouldn't have gone to the opening if she hadn't been paid to cover it for the *North Side Review*.

Standing there in a haze induced by exhaustion, cheap Chablis, and whatever nutrition came from Brie on rice cakes, Galena saw her first frost painting. It was a feathery, crystalline abstraction on glass—almost an image, like an elusive memory. It had been taken from its refrigeration box and set in a wooden stand for display, and the overheated gallery air was beginning to melt it. She stood and watched as the painting slowly turned to water from the outside in. She couldn't figure out why she found it so moving till someone behind her said, "That's how I feel." Galena realized it was how *she* felt, too—like a fragile thing being destroyed bit by bit, aging and perishing as everyone stood and watched. She stared until the painting was no more than a sheet of glass covered with tears, and all that was left was a memory of beauty that had changed and passed on, like time and lost youth.

She asked the gallery owner about the artist, and he said, "Oh, you've *got* to meet Thea. She's simply an angel. All her work is perishable, you know. She works with the craziest things—sand, smoke, ice, sparks."

Thea was dressed in an oversized lumberjack shirt and jeans, her tangled, brown hair falling around her shoulders. At first Galena wondered what kind of schtick this was; but a look at Thea's young face immediately told her that it was no schtick—the girl was simply unaware of the impression she made. Galena was suddenly seized with an urge to cherish this wisp of smoke, to protect it from all the winds that might dissipate it, to keep it young forever.

She gave Thea a ride home that night. The artist was living in a squalid, firetrap loft with five others, sleeping on old mattresses and cooking on a portable grill. The next morning, Galena bustled to the rescue, transplanting Thea into her apartment. The girl came willingly enough, but without the gratitude Galena had expected. She had yet to learn that Thea was oblivious to her environment, existing like an air plant with no soil, just on sunlight and inspiration.

Galena made the nest, brought in the money, and kept out the world. Thea brought into her life almost-forgotten pleasures like scented soaps and silk pajamas, pearly Christmas ornaments, and pomegranate seeds. Their relationship had all the hallmarks of permanence: an adopted cat, Chinese takeout in front of the television, Saturday morning errands, repainting the bedroom, bike rides in the park. Life was so nor-

Galena said, "I thought the Dirigo looked like strings of Christmas lights." That was how *Unsolved Mysteries* had it, at any rate. "No one ever said they left turds."

The woman drew another object from the case and cradled it in her palm. It was the color of a kidney, and shaped a little like one. Its surface was slick, as if wet. "The aliens didn't leave these. The people that let them take over did."

So this was the much-publicized art created by the Windrow Mountain colony. It was not up to Thea's standards. Galena felt partly relief, partly anger that Thea could have been hoodwinked into participating in this travesty.

The woman's mineralized skin did not show a flicker of emotion. "You going up there?" she said.

"Yes. I've got a friend there."

"You think. There's nothing human living up there."

There's nothing much human down here either, Galena wanted to say; but she curbed her tongue.

When she emerged from the shop, a wind brushed by, scented with sage. She turned to look south, where the Windrow Mountains still hovered like an unkept promise on the horizon. "Don't leave, kid," she whispered. "I'm coming."

The reports from Montana had fascinated Thea from the start. There were many versions from the beginning. Remote Montana community taken over by aliens. Demonic possession in Montana wasteland. Mystery Montana disease baffles scientists. Galena scoffed at it all.

After anthropologists at the University of Montana began to investigate, the explanations still metamorphosed to suit every paranoia. It was a type of mass hysteria. It was a scandalous case of environmental contamination. It was genetic inbreeding. It was a secret government experiment. One debunking journalist concluded that the "victims" were in fact members of a harmless New Age religious community who were being stigmatized by society as "ill" for their nonconformity.

The explanation of the victims themselves never changed. The Dirigo, they said, were enabling them to create art of a type never before imagined.

It was the art that riveted Thea's attention. As pictures finally filtered out, Thea bought all the magazines and pored over them. "Just think," she said, "I could work in real wind, real lightning, if I had their inspiration."

"If you had their inspiration, you'd be in a looney bin," Galena said.

But it did seem as if Thea's creativity was lagging that spring. Her studio was cluttered with unfinished work; it was over a year since she had held one of her famous shows that drew crowds to see the self-destroying art. As her comfort increased it seemed her drive faded. Galena worried that her own happiness was poisoning the well from which it sprang.

One morning when Galena, ready to leave for work, leaned over the bed to kiss her partner goodbye, Thea looked up out of the rumpled bedclothes and said, "I'm going to Montana." Galena laughed, brushed the scattered hair out of Thea's face, and said, "Ride 'em, cowboy."

When she got home that evening, Thea's suitcase and backpack were waiting by the door. The truth smashed all the elaborate structure of Galena's security. Contentment had come to her so late, so unexpectedly, that she had never thought it, too, could be perishable. She followed Thea around the house, asking questions in a voice like a lost child.

"How can I get in touch with you?"

"What are you going to do there?"

"How long will you be gone?"

"Why are you doing this?"

"When will you know?"

"What about me?"

"What about me?"

To which Thea could only answer again and again, "I don't know."

And that was all Galena had ever gotten out of her. She consented to drop Thea off at the airport, but wouldn't go in with her, and they didn't part with a kiss, or even a hug.

The road deteriorated as it began to climb. The shoulders were first to go, then the paint, till all that was left was a line of asphalt about as flat as a strip of cooked bacon. Galena's stomach was running on empty, but a touch of nervous nausea kept her from stopping to eat the granola bars she had brought. She didn't know how she was going to find Thea, and she didn't want to be wandering the Windrow Mountains all night.

The mountains wore a skirt of pine forest. The road veered to and fro through the still trunks till Galena began to suspect it didn't know where it was going. Down under the canopy of needles the air was dark as twilight, though the sun had to be in the sky, somewhere.

She rounded a corner and laid on the brakes. Ahead, the road was blocked by a fallen tree. A large yellow sign said, PRIVATE PROPERTY. TRESPASSERS WILL BE PROSECUTED. The sign was pockmarked with bullet holes.

She got out to survey the problem. The air was surprisingly cool; she must have climbed in altitude. The tree turned out to be just a poplar sapling, more leaves than trunk, felled by a chain saw. She seized a branch and dragged it across the asphalt, out of the way.

"If you want to keep me out, you'll have to try harder than this," Galena said to the unknown woodsman.

The effort had winded her, and she sat sideways in the driver's seat a while, her door open on the chill, quiet air. At first she thought that her tired eyes were playing tricks; but no, the shifting points of light were real. Off in the forest, down the winding corridors of pines, some people were carrying candles, or flashlights.

"Excuse me," Galena called out, getting up. "Can you give me some directions?"

The lights winked out. Piney silence surrounded her. Only then did Galena remember the reports—floating strings of lights sighted; gauzy veils, unexplained. She realized she was standing with one arm outstretched, as if hailing a cab. With a nervous laugh at her own absurdity, she headed back to the car and the security of self-examination. One's first brush with the paranormal ought to have more dignity than this, she decided. In her mind she composed the headlines. CHICAGOAN TRIES TO CATCH RIDE ON UFO: "I THOUGHT IT WAS A CAB," CITY SLICKER SAYS.

The road plunged down a ravine, then abruptly emerged from the trees into a barren valley. The setting sun touched the sandstone cliffs, a vivid orange. Lines of erosion made the rock face look like an ancient bas-relief, so worn away that the original sculpture was barely visible. Galena stopped the car to study it. She could almost see figures in motion—no, an inscription in flowing characters. It reminded her vividly of something. It was on the tip of her tongue: she would remember in a second.

It was just a cliff. Frowning at the illusion that had drawn her briefly out of herself, she put the car in Drive again and followed the winding road down into the heart of the valley. Rock formations rose on either side: twisted sandstone pillars that looked like figures hidden in stone cocoons, their proto-limbs still obscure beneath the surface. They drew her eyes, as if subconsciously she knew what shapes lay beneath. The valley floor held an army of them in a thousand poses, straining to free themselves. Galena sped through them; they towered over the little car, their shadows lying like barriers across the road.

At last the forest enclosed her again. It was dark now; she turned on the headlights. There was still no sign of any colony—no sign of humans at all. The last motel she had passed was just after noon.

At last, a light shone through the trees. She slowed, then spotted the driveway—just a dirt track, really. As she drove up it, the tall grass swished against the car's undercarriage.

It was a log house, probably built as a hunter's lodge. Leaving the headlights on, Galena skirted the stack of firewood and climbed three board steps onto the porch. The screen door creaked when she opened it to knock. It was several seconds before there was any response. Then, hesitantly, the door opened a crack and someone peered out.

It was Thea. "Hi there, kid," Galena said, as if she'd known it was going to be her.

Thea stood staring. "Galena," she said.

Her long brown hair fell in curly tendrils, uncombed but fetching. She looked more thin and waiflike than ever in a flannel shirt and jeans. Her feet were bare. Galena wanted to hug her to make sure that everything was all right, but there was something in her manner—a slight shrinking back, a wariness.

Thea held the door open. "Come in."

The kitchen table was soon strewn with the snapshots Galena had brought—mostly their cat, Pesto, doing assorted catlike things. Thea stared for a long time at one where the flashbulb made the cat's eyes light up like headlights.

"He's gotten to be a real sentimental slob," Galena said. "After you left, he wandered around the house and cried for a few days." So did I, she didn't say.

"Mr. Garavelli at the dry cleaners told me to say hi to you," she continued the patter she'd tried to keep up ever since entering, afraid of what silence might mean. "They've been repaving the street out front, and it's been unbearable all summer: nothing but dust and noise. Workers leaving their shirts on the bushes. Manly sweat everywhere." She took a sip of the tea that was virtually all Thea could offer her; the refrigerator was almost empty. "I had to go in to Dr. Hamer for a biopsy last week. I find out the results Tuesday."

At last Thea's eyes focused on her. "What's wrong?" she asked.

"Getting old, that's what's wrong." *Getting old alone*, she thought. *No one to tell how it feels, no one to give a damn.* "Never mind," she said.

At last silence fell. Inside the wood stove, a log settled with a brittle sound.

"Galena, I can't come back," Thea said. Her voice sounded like a guilty child confessing. "I've made the commitment here."

"Sure. I understand," Galena said, barely hearing the words. "What's important is your work. How's it going?" She glanced around the cabin. There was not a sign of artistry anywhere, just worn Salvation Army furniture.

"I'm working outside now," Thea said. "I'll show you tomorrow, if you want."

"Yes. I want."

Silence again.

"I'd better get my suitcase out of the car," Galena said. There was a twinge of pain as she rose, mocking her. *Think you're brave, do you?* it said. She took care not to react. She couldn't bear to seem vulnerable.

"Sure. You can sleep on the couch," Thea said.

Galena looked at her silently. Thea wouldn't meet her eyes. "What is this, Montana morality?" Galena asked.

"No." Thea's voice was pleading. "I just can't, Galena. I don't want you to lure me back. It will be too hard."

Too hard on whom? Galena wondered. "Okay," she said slowly. "You make the rules."

Suddenly, Thea gave her an impulsive hug. "Thank you," she whispered. As she disappeared behind the bedroom door she glanced back. The light caught her eyes with an odd glint, as if the retinas were brushed metal. For a moment she looked utterly alien.

That night Galena lay alone on the lumpy couch, kept awake by wind in the branches outside, the skittering of small feet across the roof, insect wings on the window screen. None of the soporific sounds she was used to—the roar of garbage trucks, the wail of sirens. No comforting weight of possessive cat on her feet. She wondered if Thea were awake.

This desire to be held and comforted was childish, she told herself. *You're an adult now. You know how to survive.*

Lying in the dark, she imagined a tumor growing inside her, a living thing that wasn't her, like the child she never had nor wanted. Nature had a way of getting back at people who didn't follow its rules. And reproduction was the first rule, the evolutionary imperative.

She had never made a decision to swear off men—just drifted into it, the path of least resistance. Her last attempt at a straight relationship had been a madcap fling with a sculptor. The only time they had had sex together, while she was still basking in the afterglow, he had smiled at her and said, "You look like a woman who's just been fucked."

The statement had jarred her. Why was it *she* that had just been fucked, and not *him*? He had slipped, and revealed the real reason he had done it—not for the enjoyment, no strings attached, but in order to transform her into something she hadn't been before, as if she had been raw material he had made into something. As if he had put his mark on her, like a dog pissing on a lamppost.

From that moment she knew that for men, sex was inextricably connected to power, and always would be. No matter what they said, or how enlightened they acted, sex was dominance to them, on such an instinctual, hardwired, brainstem level they could never overcome it. And she had far too vivid a sense of her own individuality to ever imagine herself as a thing marked as a man's territory.

Thea's love had always been free of other agendas. It had never been mixed up with power, or pride, or self. It had been a spontaneous gift, unpremeditated, as if it sprang from the air between them. Galena had never had to give up being who she was in order to be who Thea loved.

She hugged the pillow to the hollow feeling in her body, wondering if loneliness caused cancer.

In the morning, Galena ate a breakfast of granola bars and tea; Thea was not hungry. By daylight, the cabin looked more dilapidated than ever. One of the kitchen windows was broken, and there was an old mouse nest in a corner. "How did you find this place?" Galena asked.

"Everyone stays here when they first come," Thea answered. "It's where you wait."

"Wait for what?"

"For the Dirigo. I'll be moving on soon."

"On to where?"

"The colony. I'm almost ready."

"Will you show me the colony?"

"If you want."

Thea set out as if to walk, but Galena asked how far it was, then persuaded her to take the car. Thea looked at the Hyundai as if she'd forgotten how they worked, then opened the door awkwardly. Galena watched her carefully, suspicious.

"What do you want to see first?" Thea asked.

"What's the choice?"

"There are work sites all around us. The Wind Clock, the Haunt, Nostra Knob."

"What have you been working on?"

"The Flens."

"Let's see it, then."

A few miles down the road, Thea suddenly exclaimed, "Stop! Stop here!"

Galena pulled over. They were high on the mountainside; on their right hand was a steep drop-off, giving them a wide view of a wooded valley that wound into blue distance, interrupted by the out-thrusting roots of mountains on either side.

"Look out there," Thea said. "Do you see the painting?"

The vegetation on north slopes, south slopes, and valley floor was a pattern of green, teal, and umber. It was as if someone had taken a giant brush and painted the land to form an abstract of overlapping tints. "Isn't that natural?" Galena said.

"Of course not. This was one of the first landscape paintings the colony did. Here, let me drive so you can watch."

A little reluctantly, Galena got out and went to the passenger side. Thea said, "Unfocus your eyes just a little," then started the car slowly forward.

At first Galena saw a complex patchwork of sunny streaks. Then, as her perspective changed, a dark, spear-shaped wedge began to push its way into the foliage colors. As it touched each band of color, that area went suddenly dark, drab, and uniform. It had almost reached the opposite side when a cascade of rust, sienna, and lemon erupted from the spear tip and turned the landscape bright again.

The car stopped. Galena blinked out at the view, which had been transformed by traveling 300 feet along the road. "How did they do that?" she asked. "By painting the back side of every leaf?"

"I don't know," Thea said. "It looks different at every time of day, and every type of weather."

Galena shook her head. "Landscape painting. I see what you mean. Not painting the landscape, but *painting the landscape*. How many people did it take?"

"I don't know," Thea said again.

As they continued on, Galena looked on every prospect around her with new attention, to find more *trompes l'oeil* hidden in the leaves.

They arrived at the Flens down a rocky path. At first, it looked like a range of rampart cliffs, formed into organ-pipe pillars of a thousand dimensions. A swarm of people was at work on the cliff face, some on scaffolding anchored into the rock, some swinging on ropes. Though she tried from several angles, Galena could not tell what the sculpture was going to be.

When she asked, Thea laughed. "The sculpture is not in the rock," she said. "The medium we are working in is wind. At sunset, the mountain above us cools faster than the valley, and a wind rushes down the slope. The Flens will catch it in a thousand fissures, and part it, till it forms a shape. We will know we have gotten it right when the rock pipes sing. It's almost done; we are tuning it now."

"You are making an organ from the mountain," Galena said, struck by the strangeness of the concept.

"An organ only the wind can play," Thea answered.

As Galena watched, the workers vacated one area. There was a puff of smoke, then an echoing explosion.

"They use dynamite?" Galena asked.

"We use anything that will do the job," Thea answered.

The workers moved back into the dynamited area, their movements efficient and coordinated. Galena could see no one in charge, hear no shouted orders.

"Who designs the artworks?" she asked. "Who is in charge?"

Thea looked at the ground and shrugged.

"Thea?" Galena said.

"You will just misinterpret it," Thea said.

"Try me. Come on."

"The colonists just *know* what to do. They feel what's right. Imagine having the skill to produce each effect deliberately. Imagine thinking, 'I need pathos here, or an ominous effect,' and knowing exactly what you have to do to create it, as if it were being whispered in your ear. And everyone else knows the same."

"Kind of like having a muse?"

"That's right. The Dirigo are our muses."

Gently, Galena said, "You never needed to use anyone else's inspiration before. You never worked by anyone else's plan. That's what made you so good."

Nervously, Thea brushed a strand of hair behind her ear. "I was never as good as you thought I was."

Galena was about to protest strenuously, but Thea said, "You blew me up so big, nothing I could do would ever justify it. Everyone's expectations were so high."

"Thea, kid, you deserved it!" Galena said.

"You see what I mean," Thea said, then turned back toward the car.

"So is that my sin?" Galena shouted after her. "Having faith in you?"

Thea didn't stop or answer. When they both got back to the car they sat a while in silence. Galena considered, and rejected, half a dozen strategies: conciliatory, wounded, encouraging, authoritative. None of them were sufficient to the way she felt.

When Thea finally spoke, it wasn't about Galena at all. "Here, no one makes the art for any reason but because we want to."

They drove on to other sites. The art was everywhere. It was fashioned from streams and sand, shadows, lichen, and rain. In one place a flight of swallows was an intermittent part of the sculpture. After a while it was impossible to see the landscape as a backdrop, an accidental thing.

"Supposing these Dirigo were real—" Galena started.

"They *are* real," Thea said.

"Okay, okay. Are they trying to tell us something?"

"I don't know. You're the one who gets messages from art."

"Do they talk to you?"

"No. Not the way you mean. We don't know what they want. We're not even sure they know we're any different from the trees and rocks. Except—"

"Yes?"

"Some people feel they're trying to remember something. Something they once knew long, long ago, but now they've forgotten."

"Like us all," Galena said.

The last site they visited was what Thea called the Pivotary. They drove up a long gravel road that climbed past the trees into a cold, bleached world where the very air seemed purified and rare. Through the afternoon an ache had been growing somewhere between Galena's back and gut; when they reached the end of the road she parked and sat a while, waiting for it to subside. The sun was low, but above them the sky was still bright.

They walked side by side up a gravelly path that curved between two spurs standing out from the mountain like rock gates. Beyond them, in a sheer-sided bowl, lay a mountain lake, its surface so perfectly still it mirrored every rock around it. When they came to a halt beside it, and their footsteps ceased, silence settled in. The air seemed so crystalline it might break at a touch.

In a hushed voice, Thea said, "This is where the Dirigo live. They've been here for eons, maybe since the beginning. It's possible that the Blackfeet Indians knew about them. We think other humans may have known, once, in other times and places. We come here to invite them in. Don't worry, they can't inhabit anyone who is unwilling. You would have to go into the lake to make them part of your life."

"Like a baptism?" Galena said.

"That's right."

There was a silence. At last Thea said hesitantly, "You could do it, too. You could join us."

"Oh, Thea. When will you learn? I don't have the talent for art."

"You could. There are people in the colony who never made a thing before coming here."

"So that's what the Dirigo offer? Instant talent?"

"Vision. Creativity. A feel for the elements. If that's talent."

"What a deal," Galena said, stirring a pebble at her feet. "You'd have to be crazy to turn it down." She glanced sidelong at Thea. "But what's the catch?"

"There are only catches in a human context. Catches belong to the outside world."

"The human world, you mean. Catches are part of being human."

"All right," Thea said. "The catch is, I have to hurt you, by leaving you behind."

They stood looking at each other then—communicating, Galena thought, for the first time, though not a word was said. *I need to say it aloud*, Galena thought. *I have to admit how badly I need her.*

As the light shifted with the setting sun, it caught Thea's eyes, and the retinas reflected through, opaque as mirrors, beautiful as gemstones. A chill went down Galena's spine. She grasped Thea's hand. It felt cold.

"Have you already gone into the lake?" she asked.

Thea nodded. "Three weeks ago."

"Can you still back out?"

"I don't want to."

She was the same, but unknowable. Unchanged, yet wholly different. "What did I do to make you want this?" Galena said.

"It has nothing to do with you."

It couldn't be true, Galena thought. Somehow, this was her fault.

"Look!" Thea said, pointing out over the lake. "They've come."

The sun had set, and darkness leaped up from the ground. But the sky was still light, and the lake, reflecting it, glowed azure in the twilight. Above it, a constellation of sparks danced, firefly lights cavorting. Around them the air shimmered as with heat waves. Galena glimpsed something like a shred of iridescent gauze, gone as soon as she focused on it.

"What are they doing here?" Galena whispered. "What do they want?"

"The art," Thea said. "It's all they want. To make beautiful things. They can't do it themselves; they need our hands, our ingenuity."

She was gazing at them entranced. *I am losing her*, Galena thought.

The valley was growing dark; now faint streaks of colored light flashed and disappeared above the lake, like an aurora, or a reflection from a light that wasn't there.

Galena took Thea's hand firmly in hers. "Come on," she said, "I'll drive you home."

Following the headlights down the steep road, Galena remembered how, in the days when Thea had still gone down to her old studio to work, Galena had picked her up after work, to drive home. Sometimes she would climb the steps and hear the artists who shared the space laughing together uproariously, like teenagers. When she entered the room, the laughter would cut off self-consciously. Even if she told them to go on talking, the atmosphere would turn stiff and formal, as if Teacher were watching. It had made Galena hate to go there after a while, just to feel out of place, unwanted.

There was an ache in her gut that said, *No more future, no more chances.* Always the future had been there, a sketchbook where she could try out new scenarios. Now experimentation was done; only action was left.

She came to the main road, then retraced the way back past the turnoff to the Flens, past the landscape painting, speeding faster with every mile. As pine trunks flashed by in the darkness, Thea said, "That was the turnoff to the house. You missed it."

"I know," Galena said.

The road curved and plunged downwards, into the valley of the stone shapes. Thea said tensely, "Stop, Galena. I can't leave."

"Yes, you can," Galena said. "And I think you'd better, before they've brainwashed you completely."

She pressed down on the gas, wanting to get past the rock formations that loomed in frozen motion over the road. The passenger-side door opened, and Galena heard the pavement rushing past. She reached over to grab Thea's arm, only to feel it pull away. The loony girl was actually going to jump. Galena braked hard, and the car slewed around on loose gravel. For a moment she had a terrifying out-of-control feeling. Then the car came to rest in the roadway, facing back the way it had come. The headlight beams pointed crookedly into the dust and exhaust. The passenger seat was empty.

Galena left the car door open and walked down the harsh beams of light, searching the shoulders for a sign, her stomach muscles clenched. Then, ahead on the roadway, she saw Thea's silhouette, walking steadily away from her. She sprinted to catch up.

"Thea!" She grasped the girl's arm and forced her to turn around. "Are you—" The headlights caught Thea's eyes and they shone back, bright and preternatural.

Instinctively, Galena stepped back. Then a desperate sense that she was losing overcame her, and she grasped Thea by the shoulders. "Fight them, Thea! Don't surrender, don't let them control you. Be yourself."

A wan smile crossed Thea's face, too wise and knowing for her young features. "Myself?"

"Yes." Galena clutched her tight. "The Thea I knew."

Thea's voice was maddeningly adult. "The Thea you invented, you mean. I know all about being dominated, Galena."

Galena loosed her grip, deeply stung. "That's not true! All I ever wanted was for you to be yourself."

"Then let me go," Thea said.

"Not to give up your freedom," Galena said stubbornly. "Not to become something that's not even human."

"The only humanity I lose is the ability to make things ugly."

"Oh, isn't that great," Galena said, bitingly sarcastic. "Why don't we all join the Dirigo, then, and have a world of people who want nothing but beauty. A world of saints and artists."

"Why not?" Thea said.

There was a cloud of sparks around her head, like a halo in a medieval painting, but they cast no light on her features. Half to them and half to her Galena said, "Because it wouldn't be a human world, Thea."

There was a silence. The rock shapes around them seemed to be listening. "Then I don't want to be human," Thea said.

She was leaving her face, retreating back behind those eyes that revealed nothing. When she turned again to walk into the dark, there was no one left to stop.

The shoal of silver slivers that had hung above Thea's head did not leave with her. They still hung in the air, darting about in school formation.

Galena knew that she too could wear a halo of stars if she only consented. There was a heavy lump inside her gut—her own inhabiting being, eating her away from inside.

"Get out of here!" she shouted at the pinprick lights above her. "Let us be! You've got no business trying to make us better than we are."

Her footsteps sounded heavy and corporeal as she walked back to the car. When she had turned it around she paused with her foot on the brake, caught on a snag of grief. For a moment she rested her forehead on the steering wheel, then shifted blindly into Drive.

She had her comebacks ready by the time she got to Williston. When the car dealer's eyebrows cast aspersions her way, she said, "The Dirigo didn't want me. I guess they saw I was already alienated enough."

She would have been ashamed to commit a pun in Chicago, but this was North Dakota.

The sweaty, overly familiar salesman in the seat next to her on the plane found out where she had been and said jocularly, "Did you see any aliens?"

"Not as many as I've seen since coming back," Galena retorted.

As they circled high above the fumes and grime of O'Hare, caught in traffic, she looked down at the barren mess humanity had made of the landscape and imagined it all melting away like one of Thea's frost paintings.

It would never happen. If humanity were offered salvation on a silver platter, someone would probably just mug the messenger.

She shifted, feeling the bed of nails beneath her.

Okanoggan Falls

The town of Okanoggan Falls lay in the folded hills of southwestern Wisconsin—dairy country, marbled with deciduous groves and pastureland that looked soft as a sable's fur. It was an old sawmill town, hidden down in a steep river valley, shaded by elderly trees. Downtown was a double row of brick and ironwork storefronts running parallel to the river. Somehow, the town had steered between the Scylla and Charybdis of the franchise and the boutique. If you wanted to buy a hamburger on Main Street, you had to go to Earl's Cafe, and for scented soap there was just Meyer's Drugstore. In the park where the Civil War soldier stood, in front of the old Town Hall infested with pigeons, Mr. Woodward still defiantly raised the United States flag, as if the world on cable news were illusion, and the nation were still reality.

American small towns had changed since the days when Sinclair Lewis savaged them as backwaters of conformist complacency. All of that had moved to the suburbs. The people left in the rural towns had a high kook component. There were more welders-turned-sculptors per capita than elsewhere, more self-employed dollmakers, more wildly painted cars, more people with pronounced opinions, and more tolerance for all the above.

Like most of the Midwest, Okanoggan Falls had been relatively unaffected by the conquest and occupation. Few there had even seen one of the invading Wattesoons, except on television. At first, there had been some stirrings of grassroots defiance, born of wounded national pride; but when the Wattesoons had actually lowered taxes and still fixed the potholes, the volume of complaints had gone down. People still didn't love the occupiers, but as long as the Wattesoons minded their own business and left the populace alone, they were tolerated.

All of that changed one Saturday morning when Margie Silengo, who lived in a mobile home on Highway 14, came racing into town with her shockless Chevy bouncing like a rocking horse, telling everyone she met that a Wattesoon army convoy had gone rolling past her house and turned into the old mill grounds north of town as if they meant to stay. Almost simultaneously, the mayor's home phone rang, and Tom Abernathy found himself standing barefoot in his kitchen, for the first time in his life talking to a Wattesoon captain, who in precise, formal English informed him that Okanoggan Falls was slated for demolition.

Tom's wife Susan, who hadn't quite gotten the hang of this "occupation" thing, stopped making peanut butter sandwiches for the boys to say, "They can't say that! Who do they think they are?"

Tom was a lanky, easygoing fellow, all knobby joints and bony jaw. Mayor wasn't his full-time job; he ran one of the more successful businesses in town, a wholesale construction-goods supplier. He had become mayor the way most otherwise sensible people end up in charge: out of self-defense. Fed up with having to deal with the calcified fossil who had run the town since the 1980s, Tom had stood for office on the same impulse that occasionally led him to swear—and woke to find himself elected in a landslide, 374 to 123.

Now he rubbed the back of his head, as he did whenever perplexed, and said, "I think the Wattesoons can do pretty much anything they want."

"Then we've got to make them stop wanting to mess with us," Susan said.

That, in a nutshell, was what made Tom and Susan's marriage work. In seventeen years, whenever he had said something couldn't be done, she had taken it as a challenge to do it.

But he had never expected her to take on alien invaders.

Town council meetings weren't formal, and usually a few people straggled in late. This day, everyone was assembled at Town Hall by 5:00, when the Wattesoon officer had said he would address them. By now they knew it was not just Okanoggan Falls; all four towns along a fifty-mile stretch of Highway 14 had their own occupying forces camped outside town and their own captains addressing them at precisely 5:00. Like most Wattesoon military actions, it had been flawlessly coordinated.

The captain arrived with little fanfare. Two sand-colored army transports sped down Main Street and pulled up in front of Town Hall. The two occupants of one got out, while three soldiers in the other stood guard to keep the curious at arms' length. Their weapons remained in their slings. They seemed to be trying to keep the mood low-key.

The two who entered Town Hall looked exactly like Wattesoons on television—squat lumps of rubbly khaki-colored skin, like blobs of clay mixed with gravel. They wore the usual beige army uniforms that hermetically encased them, like shrink wrap, from neck to heel, but neither officer had on the face mask or gloves the invaders usually wore while dealing with humans. An aroma like baking rocks entered the room with them—not unpleasant, just not a smell ordinarily associated with living creatures.

In studied, formal English the larger Wattesoon introduced himself as Captain Groton and his companion as Ensign Agush. No one offered to shake hands, knowing the famous Wattesoon horror at touching slimy human flesh.

The council sat silent behind the row of desks they used for hearings, while the captain stood facing them where people normally gave testimony, but there was no question about where the power lay. The townspeople had expected gruff, peremptory orders, and so Captain Groton's reasonable tone came as a pleasant surprise; but there was nothing reassuring about his message.

The Wattesoons planned to strip-mine a fifty-mile swathe of the hilly, wooded Okanoggan Valley. "Our operations will render the land uninhabitable," Captain Groton said. "The army is here to assist in your removal. We will need you to coordinate the arrangements so this move can be achieved expeditiously and peacefully." There was the ever-so-slight hint of a threat in that last word.

When he finished there was a short silence as the council absorbed the proposed destruction of everything they had lived for and loved. The image of Okanoggan Valley transformed into a mine pit hovered before every eye: no maple trees, no lilacs, no dogs, no streetlights. Rob Massey, the scrappy newspaper editor, was first to find his voice. "What do you want to mine?" he said sharply. "There are no minerals here."

"Silica," the captain answered promptly. "There is a particularly pure bed of it underneath your limestone."

He meant the white, friable sandstone—useless for building, occasionally used for glass. What they wanted it for was incomprehensible, like so much about them. "Will we be compensated for our property?" Paula Sanders asked, as if any compensation would suffice.

"No," the captain answered neutrally. "The land is ours."

Which was infuriating, but unarguable.

"But it's our home!" Tom blurted out. "We've lived here, some of us four, five generations. We've built this community. It's our life. You can't just walk in and level it."

The raw anguish in his voice made even Captain Groton, lump of rubble that he was, pause. "But we can," he answered without malice. "It is not within your power to stop it. All you can do is reconcile yourselves to the inevitable."

"How much time do we have?" Paula bit her words off as if they tasted bad.

"We realize you will need time to achieve acceptance, so we are prepared to give you two months."

The room practically exploded with protests and arguments.

At last the captain held up the blunt appendage that served him as a hand. "Very well," he said. "I am authorized to give you an extension. You may have three months."

Later, they learned that every captain up and down the valley had given the same extension. It had obviously been planned in advance.

The room smoldered with outrage as the captain turned to leave, his job done. But before he could exit, Susan Abernathy stepped into the doorway, along with the smell of brewing coffee from the hall outside.

"Captain Groton," she said, "would you like to join us for coffee? It's a tradition after meetings."

"Thank you, madam," he said, "but I must return to base."

"Susan," she introduced herself and, contrary to all etiquette, held out her hand.

The Wattesoon recoiled visibly. But in the next second he seemed to seize control of himself and, by sheer force of will, extended his arm. Susan clasped it warmly, looking down into his pebbly eyes. "Since we are going to be neighbors, at least for the next few months, we might as well be civil," she said.

"That is very foresighted of you, madam," he answered.

"Call me Susan," she said. "Well, since you can't stay tonight, can I invite you to dinner tomorrow?"

The captain hesitated, and everyone expected another evasion, but at last he said, "That would be acceptable. Susan."

"Great. I'll call you with the details." As the captain left, followed closely by his ensign, she turned to the council. "Can I bring you some coffee?"

"Ish. What did it feel like?" said her son Nick.

Susan had become something of a celebrity in the eleven-year-old set for having touched an alien.

"Dry," she said, staring at the laptop on the dining room table. "A little lumpy. Kind of like a lizard."

In the next room, Tom was on the phone. "Warren, you're talking crazy," he said. "We still might be able to get some concessions. We're working on it. But if you start shooting at them, we're doomed. I don't want to hear any more about toad hunts, okay?"

"Have you washed your hand?" Nick wanted to know.

Susan let go of the mouse to reach out and wipe her hand on Nick's arm. "Eew, gross!" he said. "Now I've got toad germs."

"Don't call them that," she said sharply. "It's not polite. You're going to have to be very polite tonight."

"I don't have to touch him, do I?"

"No, I'm sure touching a grody little boy is the last thing he wants."

In the next room, Tom had dialed a different number. "Listen, Walt, I think I'm going to need a patrol car in front of my house tonight. If this toad gets shot coming up my walk, my house is going to be a smoking crater tomorrow."

"Is that true?" Nick asked, wide-eyed.

"No," Susan lied. "He's exaggerating."

"Can I go to Jake's tonight?"

"No, I need you here," Susan said, hiding the pang of anxiety it gave her.

"What are we having for dinner?"

"I'm trying to find out what they eat, if you'd just leave me alone."

"I'm not eating bugs."

"Neither am I," Susan said. "Now go away."

Tom came in and sank into a chair with a sigh. "The whole town is up in arms," he said. "Literally. Paula wanted to picket our house tonight. I told her to trust you, that you've got a plan. Of course, I don't know what it is."

"I think my plan is to feed him pizza," Susan said.

"Pizza?"

"Why not? I can't find that they have any dietary restrictions, and everyone loves pizza."

Tom laid his head back and stared glumly at the ceiling. "Sure. Why not? If it kills him, you'll be a hero. For about half an hour; then you'll be a martyr."

"Pizza never killed anyone," Susan said, and got up to start straightening up the house.

The Abernathys lived in a big old 1918 three-story with a wraparound porch and a witch's-hat tower, set in a big yard. The living room had wood pocket-doors, stained-glass fanlights, and a wood-framed fireplace. It could have been fancy, but instead it had a frayed, lived-in look—heaps of books, puppy-chewed Oriental carpet, an upright piano piled with model airplanes. The comfy, well-dented furniture showed the marks of constant comings and goings, school projects, and meetings. There was rarely a night when the Abernathys didn't have guests, but dinner was never formal. Formality was alien to Susan's nature.

She had been an RN, but had quit, fed up with the bureaucracy rather than the patients. She had the sturdy physique of a German farm girl and the competent independence to go with it. Light brown hair, cropped just above her shoulders, framed her round, cheerful face. Only rarely was she seen in anything more fancy than a jean skirt and a shirt with rolled-up sleeves. When they had elected Tom, everyone had known they weren't getting a mayor's wife who would challenge anybody's fashion sense.

That night, Captain Groton arrived precisely on time, in a car with tinted windows, driven by someone who stayed invisible, waiting. Tom met the guest on the doorstep, looking up and down the street a little nervously. When they came into the living room, Susan emerged from the kitchen with a bouquet of wine glasses in one hand and a bottle in the other.

"Wine, Captain?" she said.

He hesitated. "If that is customary. I regret I am not familiar with your dietary rituals. I only know they are complex."

"It's fermented fruit juice, mildly intoxicating," she said, pouring a little bit in his glass. "People drink it to relax."

He took the glass gingerly. Susan saw that he had stumpy nubbin fingers. As a nurse, she had had to train herself to feel compassion even for the least appealing patients, and now she called on that skill to disregard his appearance.

"Cheers," she said, lifting her glass.

There was a snap as the stem on Captain Groton's glass broke in two. The wine slopped onto his hand as he tried to catch the pieces. "Pardon me," he mumbled. "Your vessel is brittle."

"Never mind the glass," Susan said, taking it and handing the pieces to Tom. "Did you cut yourself?"

"No, of course—" he stopped in mid-denial, staring at his hand. A thin line of blood bisected the palm.

"Here, I'll take care of that," she said. Taking him by the arm, she led him to the bathroom. It was not until she had dabbed the blood off with a tissue that she realized he was not recoiling at her touch as he had before. Inwardly, she smiled at small victories. But when she brought out a bottle of spray disinfectant, he did recoil, demanding suspiciously, "What is it?"

"Disinfectant," she said. "To prevent infection. It's alcohol-based."

"Oh," he said. "I thought it might be water."

She spritzed his hand lightly, then applied a bandage. He was looking curiously around. "What is this place?"

"It's a bathroom," she said. "We use it to—well, clean ourselves, and groom, and so forth. This is the toilet." She raised the lid, and he drew back, obviously repulsed. She had to laugh. "It's really very clean. I swear."

"It has water in it," he said with disgust.

"But the water's not dirty, not now."

"Water is always dirty," he said. "It teems with bacteria. It transmits a thousand diseases, yet you humans touch it without any caution. You allow your children to play in it. You drink it, even. I suppose you have gotten used to it, living on this world where it contaminates everything. It even falls from the sky. It is impossible to get away from it. You have no choice but to soak in it."

Struck by the startling image of water as filth, Susan said, "Occupying our world must be very unpleasant for you. What is your planet like?"

"It is very dry," he said. "Miles and miles of hot, clean sand, like your Sahara. But your population does not live in the habitable spots, so we cannot either."

"You must drink water sometimes. Your metabolisms are not that different from ours, or you would not be able to eat our food."

"The trace amounts in foods are enough for us. We do not excrete it like you do."

"So that's why you don't have bathrooms," she said.

He paused, clearly puzzled. Then it dawned on him what she had left out of her explanation. "You use this room for excretory functions?"

"Yes," she said. "It's supposed to be private."

"But you excrete fluids in public all the time," he said. "From your noses, your mouths, your skin. How can you keep it private?"

For a moment the vision of humans as oozing bags of bacteria left her unable to answer. Then she said, "That's why we come here, to clean it all off."

He looked around. "But there is no facility for cleaning."

"Sure there is." She turned on the shower. "See?"

He reacted with horror, so she quickly shut it off. She explained, "You see, we think of water as clean. We bathe in it. How do you bathe?"

"Sand," he said. "Tubs of dry, heated sand. It is heavenly."

"It must be." She could picture it: soft, white sand. Like what lay under the Okanoggan limestone. She looked at him in dawning realization. "Is that why you want…?"

"I cannot say anything about that," he said. "Please do not ask me."

Which was all the answer she needed.

When they came back out, Tom and the boys were in the kitchen, so that was where they went.

"Sorry, we got caught up in a really interesting conversation," Susan said breezily, with an I'll-tell-you-later look at Tom. "Captain Groton, these are our sons, Ben and Nick." The boys stood up and nodded awkwardly, obviously coached not to shake hands.

"They are both yours?" the Wattesoon asked.

"Yes," Tom said. "Do you have any kids, captain?"

"Yes. A daughter."

"How old is she?" Susan said, pouring some more wine for him in a mug.

Captain Groton paused so long she wondered if she had said something offensive, but finally he shook his head. "I cannot figure it out. The time dilation makes it too difficult. It would mean little to you anyway; our years are so different."

"So she's back home on your planet?"

"Yes."

"Your wife, too?"

"She is dead."

"I'm so sorry. It must have been hard for you to leave your daughter behind."

"It was necessary. I was posted here. I followed my duty."

It had occurred to Susan that perhaps cow-excretion pie was not the thing to offer her guest, so she began rummaging in the cupboard, and soon assembled a buffet of dry foods: roast soybeans, crackers, apple chips, pine nuts, and a sweet potato for moisture. As Tom tried valiantly to engage the captain in a conversation about fishing, she started assembling the pizza for her family. The dog was barking at the back door, so she asked Ben to feed him. Nick started playing with his Gameboy. There was a pleasantly normal confusion all around.

"What sorts of food do you eat at home?" Susan asked her guest when she had a chance.

Groton shrugged. "We are less preoccupied with food than you are. Anything will do. We are omnivores."

Ben muttered, "Better watch out for our dogs."

"Ben!" Susan rebuked him.

Captain Groton turned marbly eyes on him. "We have no interest in your food animals."

The whole family stared in horror. "Our dogs aren't food!" Ben blurted.

"Then why do you keep them?" the captain asked reasonably.

Tom said, "For companionship."

Ben said, "For fun."

Susan said, "Because they remind us that we're human. Without other species around, we'd forget."

"Ah. I see," the Wattesoon said. "We feel the same."

In the awkward silence that followed, the humans all wondered who were the Wattesoons' pets.

They were saved by the timer. The pizza came out of the oven, and soon all was cheerful confusion again.

The internet had told Susan that Wattesoons were frugal eaters, but Captain Groton seemed ravenous. He ate some of everything she put on the table, including two slices of pizza.

To spare their guest the troubling sight of counters, tabletop, and utensils being smeared with water, Susan asked him out to see the back yard so the others could clean up. The screen door banged shut behind them, and the dog came trotting up, eager to smell the stranger, till Susan shooed him into the kitchen. She then led the Wattesoon out into the humid, crickety twilight.

It was a Midwestern evening. The yard backed up onto the river bluff, a weathered limestone cliff overgrown with sumac and grapevine. Susan strolled out past the scattered detritus of frisbees and lawn darts toward the quiet of the lower yard, where nature had started to encroach. There was an old swing hung from a gnarled oak tree, and she sat down in it, making the ropes creak. In the shady quiet, she swung idly to and fro, thinking of other evenings.

She had never realized how desperately she loved this place until she was forced to think of losing it. Looking toward the dark bushes by the cliff, she saw the silent flare of fireflies. "Are you able to find this beautiful?" she said, not trying to hide the longing in her voice.

After a few moments of silence, she looked over to find the captain gazing into the dark, lost in thought. "I am sorry," he said, recollecting himself. "What did you ask?"

Instead of answering, she said, "I think we each get imprinted on a certain kind of landscape when we're young. We can enjoy other spots, but only one seems like we're made from it, down to our bones. This is mine."

"Yes," he said.

"Can you understand how it is for us, then? We talk a lot about our investments and our livelihoods, but that's just to hide the pain. We love this place. We're bonded to it."

He didn't answer at once, so she stopped the swing to look at him.

"I understand," he said.

"Do you?" she said hopefully.

"It changes nothing. I am sorry."

Disappointed, she stared at his lumpy face. Now that she was a little more accustomed to him, he did not seem quite so rubbly and squat. He gave an impatient gesture. "Why are your people so fond of being discontent? You relish resisting, protesting, always pushing against the inevitable. It is an immature response, and makes your lives much harder."

"But, Captain, there are some things that *ought* to be protested."

"What things?"

"Folly. Malice. Injustice."

He cut her off in a pained tone. "These things are part of the nature of existence. There is nothing we can do to prevent them."

"You would not even try?" she said.

"Life is not just. Fairness is a fool's concept. To fight brings only disillusion."

"Well, we are different. We humans can put up with a thousand evils so long as we think they are fair. We are striving all the time to bring about justice, in ourselves and our society. Yours too, if you would let us."

"So your truculence is all an effort to improve us?" the Wattesoon said.

Surprised, Susan laughed. "Why, Captain Groton, no one told me your people had a sense of irony."

He seemed taken aback by her reaction, as if he regretted having provoked it.

"I was not laughing at you," she explained hastily. "At least, not in any way you would not wish."

"You cannot know what I would wish," he said stiffly.

She said, "Oh, I don't know about that." For the time being, here out of all official contexts, he seemed just as difficult and contradictory as any human male. Speculatively, she said, "Your answer just now, about justice. You sounded bitter, as if you spoke from some experience. What was it?"

He stared at her with that unreadable, granitic face. For a few moments she thought he wasn't going to answer. Then he said, "It is in the past. There is no point in talking about it. Today is today. I accept that."

They remained silent for a while, listening to the sounds of life all around. At last Susan said, "Well, the great injustice of *our* lives is still in the future."

The thought of it flooded into her. All of this gentle valley would be gone soon, turned into an open wound in the landscape. Tears came to her, half anger and half loss, and she got up to go back inside. When she reached the back porch, she paused to compose herself, wiping the tears from her face. Captain Groton, who had followed her, said in a startled voice, "You are secreting moisture."

"Yes," she said. "We do that from time to time, in moments of intense emotion."

"I wish—" he started, then stopped.

"Yes? What do you wish?"

"Never mind," he said, and looked away.

That night, lying in bed, she told Tom all she had learned.

"Sand," he said in disbelief. "The bastards are moving us out so they can have bathtub sand."

He was not feeling charitable toward the Wattesoons. After their dinner guest had left in his tinted limousine, Tom had gotten a call from the mayor of Walker, the closest Wal-Mart metropolis. The captain in charge of their evacuation was an unbending disciplinarian who had presented the residents with a set of non-negotiable deadlines. The news from Red Bluff was even less encouraging. The captain assigned there was a transparent racist who seemed to think evacuation was too good for the native population. Force seemed to be his preferred alternative.

"Larry wants us to mount a unified resistance," Tom said. "A kind of 'Hell no, we won't go' thing. Just stay put, refuse to prepare. It seems pretty risky to me."

Susan lay reflecting. At last she said, "They would think it was an immature response."

"What, like children disobeying?" he said, irritated.

"I didn't say I agreed. I said that was what they would think."

"So what *should* we do?"

"I don't know. Behave in a way they associate with adults. Somehow resist without seeming to resist."

Tom turned his head on the pillow to look at her. "How come you learn all these things? He won't give me anything but the official line."

"You're his counterpart, Tom. He has to be formal with you. I don't count."

"Or maybe you count more. Maybe he's sweet on you."

"Oh, please!"

"Who would've thought I'd lose my wife to a potato?" Tom mused.

She quelled the urge to hit him with a pillow. "You know, he's something of a philosopher."

"Socrates the spud," he said.

"More like Marcus Aurelius. I don't think he really wants to be here. There is something in his past, some tragedy he won't talk about. But it might make him sympathetic to us. We might win him over."

Tom rose on one elbow to look at her earnestly. "My god, he really did open up to you."

"I'm just putting two and two together. The problem is, I'm not sure what winning him over would get us. He's just following orders."

"Shit, even one friend among the Wattesoon is progress. I say go for it."

"Is that an order, Mr. Mayor?"

"My Mata Hari," he said, with the goofy, lopsided grin she loved.

She rolled closer to put her head on his shoulder. All problems seemed more bearable when he was around.

In the next few weeks, no one saw much of Captain Groton. Information, instructions, and orders still emanated from his office, but the captain himself was unavailable—indisposed, the official line went. When she heard this, Susan called the Wattesoon headquarters, concerned that he had had a reaction to the odd menu she had fed him. To her surprise, the captain took her call.

"Do not concern yourself, Susan," he said. "There is nothing you can do."

"I don't believe you," she said. "You're so in love with stoical acceptance that you could have toxic shock before you'd admit there was anything wrong."

"There is nothing wrong."

"I'm a nurse, Captain Groton. If you are sick, you have become my job."

There was an enigmatic pause on the line. "It is nothing you would recognize," he said at last. "A Wattesoon complaint."

Concerned now that he had admitted it, she said, "Is it serious?"

"It is not mortal, if that is what you mean."

"Can I see you?"

"Your concern is gratifying, but I have no need of assistance."

And she had to be content with that.

In the end, Tom saw him before she did. It was at a meeting the captain couldn't avoid, a progress report on preparations for the evacuation. "It must be some sort of arthritis," Tom answered Susan's questions vaguely. "He's hobbling around with a cane. A bit testy, too."

Not trusting a man to observe what needed to be noticed, Susan called Alice Brody, who had also been at the meeting. She was more than willing to elaborate. "He does seem to be in discomfort," Alice said. "But that's not the strange part."

Aha, Susan thought.

"He's *taller*, Susan. By inches. And proportioned differently. Not quite so tubby, if you know what I mean. It looks like he's lost a lot of weight, but I think it's just redistributed. His skin is different, too—smoother, a more natural color."

"What do you think is going on?"

"Damned if I know."

That was when Susan got the idea to invite Captain Groton to the Fourth of July celebration. Observing the holiday at all had been controversial, under the circumstances—but the city council had reasoned that a day of frivolity would raise everyone's spirits. The Wattesoons regarded it as a quaint summer festival and completely missed the nationalist connotations, so their only objection was to the potential for disorder from the crowds. When the town agreed to ban alcohol, the occupiers relented.

Okanoggan Falls' Fourth of July always climaxed with the parade, a homegrown affair for which people prepared at least three hours in advance. There was always a chainsaw drill team, a float for the Butter Princess, a Dixieland jazz band on a flatbed truck, and decorated backhoes and front-end loaders in lieu of floats. Deprecating self-mockery was a finely honed sport in Wisconsin.

Tom was going to be obliged to ride in a Model T with a stovepipe hat on, so Susan phoned the Wattesoon commander and asked him to accompany her.

"It will be a real demonstration of old-time Americana," she said.

He hesitated. "I do not wish to be provocative. Your townsfolk might not welcome my presence."

"If you were riding in a float, maybe. But mingling with the crowds, enjoying a brat and a lemonade? Some people might even appreciate it. If they don't, I'll handle them."

At last he consented, and they arranged to meet. "Don't wear a uniform," was her last instruction.

She had no idea what a dilemma she had caused him till he showed up in front of Meyer's Drugstore in a ragbag assortment of ill-fitting clothes that looked salvaged from a thrift shop. However, the truly extraordinary thing was that he was able to wear them at all—for when she had last seen him, fitting into human clothes would have been out of the question. Now, when she greeted him, she realized they were the same height, and he actually had a chin.

"You look wonderful," she blurted out.

"You are exaggerating," he said in a slightly pained tone.

"Are you feeling all right?"

"Better, thank you."

"But your clothes. Oh dear."

"Are they inappropriate?" he asked.

She looked around at all the American summer slobbery—men in baggy teeshirts and sandals, women bursting out of their tank tops. "No," she said. "You'll fit right in. It's just that, for a man in your position…" She grabbed him by the hand and dragged him into the drugstore, making for the magazine rack. She found an issue of *GQ* and thrust it into his hands. "Study that," she said. "It will show you what the elite class of men wear." Perusing several other magazines, she found some examples of a more khakified, Cape Cod look. "This is more informal, but still tasteful. Good for occasions like this, without losing face."

He was studying the pictures with a grave and studious manner. "Thank you, Susan. This is helpful." With a pang, she wished Tom would take any of her sartorial advice so to heart.

They were heading for the counter to buy the magazines when he stopped, riveted by the sight of the shelves. "What are these products for?" he asked.

"Grooming, personal care," Susan said. "These are for cleaning teeth. We do it twice a day, to prevent our breath smelling bad and our teeth going yellow. These are for shaving off unwanted hair. Men shave their faces every day, or it grows in."

"You mean all men have facial hair?" Captain Groton said, a little horrified.

"Yes. The ones who don't want beards just shave it off."

"What about these?" he said, gesturing to the deodorants.

"We spread it under our arms every day, to prevent unpleasant odors."

Faintly he said, "You live at war with your bodies."

She laughed. "It does seem that way, doesn't it?" She looked down the aisle at the shampoos, mouthwashes, acne creams, corn removers, soaps, and other products attesting to the ways in which even humans found their own bodies objectionable.

Beth Meyer was manning the counter, so Susan introduced her to Captain Groton. Unable to hide her hostility, Beth nevertheless said, "I hope you learn something about us."

"Your shop has already been very instructive, Mrs. Meyer," the captain said courteously. "I never realized the ingenuity people devote to body care. I hope I may return some day."

"As long as we're open we won't turn away a customer," Beth said.

Outside, things were gearing up for the parade, and it was clear that people were spontaneously going to use it to express their frustration. Some of the spectators were carrying protest signs, and along the sidewalk one local entrepreneur had set up a Spike the Spud concession stand offering people a chance to do sadistic things to baked potatoes for a few dollars. The most popular activity seemed to be blowing up the potatoes with firecrackers, as attested to by the exploded potato guts covering the back of the plywood booth. A reporter from an out-of-town TV station was interviewing the proprietor about his thriving business. The word "Wattesoon" never passed anyone's lips, but no one missed the point.

Including Captain Groton. Susan saw him studying the scene, so she said quietly, "It's tasteless, but better they should work it out this way than in earnest."

"That is one interpretation," he said a little tensely. She reminded herself that it wasn't *her* symbolic viscera plastering the booth walls.

His radio chose that moment to come to life. Susan hadn't even realized he was carrying it, hidden under his untucked shirt. He said, "Excuse me," and spoke into it in his own language. Susan could not tell what was being said, but the captain's voice was calm and professional. When he finished, she said, "Do you have soldiers ready to move in?"

He studied her a moment, as if weighing whether to lie, then said, "It would have been foolish of us not to take precautions."

It occurred to her then that he was their advance reconnaissance man, taking advantage of her friendship to assess the need for force against her neighbors. At first she felt a prickle of outrage; it quickly morphed into relief that he had not sent someone more easily provoked.

"Hey, captain!" The man at the Spike the Spud stand had noticed them, and, emboldened by the TV camera, had decided to create a photogenic scene. "Care to launch a spud missile?" The people standing around laughed nervously, transfixed to see the Wattesoon's reaction. Susan was drawing breath to extricate him when he put a restraining hand on her arm.

"I fear you would think me homicidal," he said in an easygoing tone.

Everyone saw then that he understood the message of sublimated violence, but chose to take it as a joke and not a provocation.

"No homicide involved, just potatoes," said the boothkeeper. He was a tubby, unshaven man in a sloppy white teeshirt. His joking tone had a slightly aggressive edge. "Come on, I'll give you a shot for free."

Captain Groton hesitated as everyone watched intently to see what he would do. At last he gave in. "Very well," he said, stepping up to the booth, "but I insist on paying. No preferential treatment."

The boothkeeper, an amateur comedian, made a show of selecting a long, thin potato that looked remarkably like his customer. He then offered a choice of weapons: sledge hammer, ax, firecracker, or other instruments of torture. "Why, the firecracker of course," the captain said. "It is traditional today, is it not?"

"American as beer." One segment of the crowd resented that the Wattesoons had interfered with their patriotic right to inebriation.

The boothkeeper handed him the potato and firecracker. "Here, shove it in. Right up its ass." When the captain complied, the man set the potato in the back of the booth and said, "Say when."

When the captain gave the word, the man lit the fuse. They waited breathlessly; then the potato exploded, splattering the boothkeeper in the face. The onlookers hooted with laughter. Captain Groton extracted himself with an amiable wave, as if he had planned the outcome all along.

"You were a remarkably good sport about that," Susan said to him as they walked away.

"I could have obliterated the tuber with my weapon," he said, "but I thought it would violate the spirit of the occasion."

"You're packing a weapon?" Susan stared. Wattesoon weapons were notoriously horrific. He could have blown away the booth and everyone around it.

He looked at her without a shade of humor. "I have to be able to defend myself."

The parade was about to commence, and Susan was feeling that she was escorting an appallingly dangerous person, so she said, "Let's find a place to stand, away from the crowd."

"Over here," Captain Groton said. He had already scoped out the terrain and located the best spot for surveillance: the raised stoop of an old apartment building, where he could stand with his back to the brick. He climbed the steps a bit stiffly, moving as if unused to knees that bent.

Okanoggan Falls had outdone itself. It was a particularly cheeky parade, full of double-entendre floats like the one carrying a group called the No Go Banjoes playing "Don't Fence Me In," or the "I Don't Wanna Mooove" banner carried by the high school cheerleading squad in their black-and-white Holstein costumes. The captain's radio kept interrupting, and he spoke in a restrained, commanding voice to whoever was on the other end.

In the end, it all passed without intervention from any soldiers other than the one at Susan's side. When the crowd began to disperse, she found that she had been clenching her fists in tension, and was glad no one else was aware of the risk they had been running.

"What happens now?" Captain Groton said. He meant it militarily, she knew; all pretense of his purpose being social was gone.

"Everyone will break up now," she said. "Some will go to the school ball field for the fund-raiser picnic, but most won't gather again till the fireworks tonight. That will be about 9:30 or 10:00."

He nodded. "I will go back to base, then."

She was battling mixed feelings, but at last said, "Captain—thank you, I think."

He studied her seriously. "I am just doing my duty."

That night on the television news, the celebration in Okanoggan Falls was contrasted with the one in Red Bluff, where a lockdown curfew was in place, fireworks were banned, and Wattesoon tanks patrolled the empty streets.

A week later, when Susan phoned Captain Groton, Ensign Agush took the call. "He cannot speak to you," he said indifferently. "He is dying."

"What?" Susan said, thinking she had heard wrong.

"He has contracted one of your human diseases."

"Has anyone called a doctor?"

"No. He will be dead soon. There is no point."

Half an hour later, Susan was at the Wattesoon headquarters with her nurse's kit in hand. When the ensign realized he was facing a woman with the determination of a storm trooper, he did not put up a fight, but showed her to the captain's quarters. He still seemed unconcerned about his commanding officer's imminent demise.

Captain Groton slumped in a chair in his spartan but private sitting room. The transformation in his appearance was even more remarkable; he was now tall and slender, even for a human, and his facial features had a distinctly human cast. He might have passed for an ordinary man in dim light.

An exceedingly miserable ordinary man. His eyes were red-rimmed, his face unshaved (she noted the facial hair with surprise), and his voice was a hoarse croak when he said, "Susan! I was just thinking I should thank you for your kindness before..." He was interrupted by a sneeze.

Still preoccupied with his appearance, she said, "You are turning human, aren't you?"

"Your microbes evidently think so." He coughed phlegm. "I have contracted an exceedingly repulsive disease."

She drew up a chair next to him. "What are your symptoms?"

He shook his head, obviously thinking the subject was not a fit one. "Don't be concerned. I am resigned to die."

"I'm asking as a professional."

Reluctantly, he said, "This body appears to be dissolving. It is leaking fluids from every orifice. There, I told you it was repulsive."

"Your throat is sore? Your nose is congested? Coughing and sneezing?"

"Yes, yes."

"My dear captain, what you have is called a cold."

"No!" he protested. "I am quite warm."

"That's probably because you have a fever." She felt his forehead. "Yes. Well, fortunately, I've brought something for that." She brought out a bottle of aspirin, some antihistamine, decongestant, and cough suppressant. She added a bottle of Vitamin C for good measure.

"You are not alarmed?" he asked hesitantly.

"Not very. In us, the disease normally cures itself in a week or so. Since your immune system has never encountered it before, I'm not sure about you. You have to level with me, captain. Have you become human in ways besides appearance?"

Vaguely, he said, "How long has it been?"

"How long has what been?"

"Since I first saw you."

She thought back. "About six weeks."

"The transformation is far advanced, then. In three weeks I will be indistinguishable from one of you."

"Internally as well?"

"You would need a laboratory to tell the difference."

"Then it should be safe to treat you as if you were human. I'll be careful, though." She looked around the room for a glass of water. "Where's your ba—" It was a Wattesoon apartment; of course there was no bathroom. By now, she knew they excreted only hard, odorless pellets. "Where can I get a glass of water?"

"What for?" He looked mildly repulsed.

"For you to drink with these pills."

"*Drink*?"

"You mean to tell me you've had no fluids?"

"We don't require them…"

"Oh, dear Lord. You're probably dehydrated as well. You're going to have to change some habits, captain. Sit right there. I need to run to the grocery store."

At the grocery she stocked up on fruit juices, bottled water, tissues, and, after a moment's hesitation, toilet paper—though not relishing having to explain that one to him. She also bought soap, a washcloth, mouthwash, shaving gel, a packet of plastic razors, a pail, and a washbasin. Like it or not, he was going to have to learn.

She had dealt with patients in every state of mental derangement, but never had she had to teach one how to be human. When she had gotten him to down the pills and a bottle of orange juice, she explained the purpose of her purchases to him in plain, practical language. She showed him how to blow his nose, and explained how a human bladder and bowel worked, and the necessity of washing with soap and water. When she finished he looked, if anything, more despairing than before.

"It is not common knowledge to us that you are hiding these bodily deficiencies," he said. "I fear I made a grave error in judgment."

"You're a soldier," she said. "Stop dramatizing and cope with it."

For a moment he stared, astonished at her commanding tone. Then she could see him marshalling his courage as if to face dismemberment and death. "You are justified to rebuke me," he said. "I chose this. I must not complain."

Soon the antihistamine was making him drowsy, so she coaxed him to return to bed. "You're best off if you just sleep," she told him. "Take more of the pills every four hours, and drink another bottle every time you wake. If you feel pressure and need to eliminate liquid, use the pail. Don't hold it in, it's very bad for you. Call me in the morning."

"You're leaving?" he said anxiously.

She had intended to, but at his disconsolate expression she relented. It made her realize that she could actually read expressions on his face now. She drew up a chair and sat. "I must say, your comrades here don't seem very sympathetic."

He was silent a few moments, staring bleakly at the ceiling. At last he said, "They are ashamed."

"Of what? You?"

"Of what I am becoming."

"A human? They're bigots, then."

"Yes. You have to understand, Susan, the army doesn't always attract the highest caliber of men."

She realized then that the drug, or the reprieve from death, had broken down his usual reticence. It put her in an odd position, to have the occupying commander relying on her in his current unguarded condition. Extracting military or political secrets would clearly violate medical ethics. But was personal and cultural information allowed? She made a snap decision: nothing that would hurt him. Cautiously, she said, "I didn't know that you Wattesoons had this…talent…ability… to change your appearance."

"It only works with a closely related species," he said drowsily. "We weren't sure you were similar enough. It appears you are."

"How do you do it?"

He paused a long time, then said, "I will tell you some day. The trait has been useful to us, in adapting to other planets. Planets more unlike our own than this one is."

"Is that why you changed? To be better adapted?"

"No. I felt it was the best way to carry out my orders."

She waited for him to explain that; when he didn't, she said, "What orders?"

"To oversee the evacuation on time and with minimal disturbance. I thought that looking like a human would be an advantage in winning the cooperation of the local populace. I wanted you to think of me as human. I did not know of the drawbacks then."

"Well, I don't think you would have fooled us anyway," Susan said a little skeptically. "Can you change your mind now?"

"No. The chameleon process is part of our reproductive biology. We cannot change our minds about that, either."

The mention of reproduction brought up something she had often wondered about. "Why are there no Wattesoon women here?" she asked.

The subject seemed to evoke some sort of intense emotion for him. In a tight voice, he said, "Our women almost invariably die giving birth. The only ones who live long, as a rule, are childless, and they are rare. If it were not for the frequency of multiple births, we would have difficulty maintaining our population. We see the ease with which you human women give birth, and envy it."

"It wasn't always this way," Susan said. "We used to die much more frequently, as well. But that wasn't acceptable to us. We improved our medicine until we solved the problem."

Softly, he said, "It is not acceptable to us, either."

A realization struck her. "Is that what happened to your wife?"

"Yes."

She studied his face. "I think you must have loved her."

"I did. Too much."

"You can't blame yourself for her death."

"Who should I blame?"

"The doctors. The researchers who don't find a cure. The society that doesn't put a high enough priority on finding a solution."

He gave a little laugh. "That is a very human response."

"Well, *we* have solved our problem."

He considered that answer so long she thought he had fallen asleep. But just as she was rising to check, he said, "I think it is better to go through life as a passer-by, detached from both the good and the bad. Especially from the good, because it always goes away."

Gently, Susan said, "Not always."

He looked at her with clouded eyes. "Always."

And then he really did fall asleep.

~

That evening, after the boys had gone up to their rooms, Susan told Tom everything over wine. Some of the medical details made him wince.

"Ouch. The poor bastard. Sounds worse than puberty, all crammed into nine weeks."

"Tom, you could really help him out," Susan said. "There are things you could tell him, man to man, that I can't—"

"Oh no, I couldn't," Tom said. "No way."

She protested, "But there are things about male anatomy—you expect *me* to warn him about all that?"

"Better you than me," Tom said.

"Coward," she said.

"Damn right. Listen, men just don't talk about these things. How am I supposed to bring it up? More to the point, why? He got himself into this. It was a military strategy. He even admitted it to you: he wanted to manipulate us to cooperate in our own conquest. I don't know why you're acting as if you're responsible for him."

Tom was right. She studied the wine in her glass, wondering at her own reaction. She had been empathizing as if Captain Groton were her patient, not her enemy. He had deliberately manipulated her feelings, and it had worked.

Well, she thought, two could play at that game.

It was not to be a summer of days at the beach, or fishing trips, or baseball camp. Everyone was busy packing, sorting, and getting ready to move. Susan marshalled Nick and Ben into the attic and basement to do the easy part, the packing and stacking, but the hardest part of moving was all hers: making the decisions. What to take, what to leave. It was a referendum on her life, sorting the parts worth saving from the rest. No object was just itself: it was memories, encapsulated in grimy old toys, birthday cards, garden bulbs, and comforters. All the tiny, pointillist moments that together formed the picture of her life. Somehow, she had to separate her self from the place that had created her, to become a rootless thing.

The summer was punctuated with sad ceremonies like the one when they started disinterring the bodies from the town cemetery, the day when the crane removed the Civil War soldier from the park, and the last church service before they took out the stained glass windows. After the dead had left, the town paradoxically seemed even more full of ghosts.

The protests did not die down. Red Bluff was in a state of open rebellion; a hidden sniper had picked off three Wattesoon soldiers, and the army was starting house-to-house searches to disarm the populace. In Walker, angry meetings were televised, in which residents shouted and wept.

In Okanoggan Falls, they negotiated. The Wattesoons were now paying to move three of the most significant historic buildings, and the school district would be kept intact after relocation. Captain Groton had even agreed to move the deadline two weeks into September so the farmers could harvest the crops—a concession the captains in Red Bluff and Walker were eventually forced to match, grudgingly.

The captain became a familiar face around town—no longer in a limousine, but driving a rented SUV to supervise contractors, meet with civic groups, or simply to stop for lunch at Earl's Cafe and chat with the waitress. Outwardly, there was no longer a hint of anything Wattesoon about him, unless it was his awkwardness when asked to tie a knot or catch a baseball. He had turned into a tall, distinguished older man with silver hair, whose manners were as impeccable as his dress. In social settings he was reserved, but occasionally something would catch his whimsy, and then he had a light, tolerant laugh. At the same time, a steely authority lay just under the surface.

The women of Okanoggan began to notice. They began to approach and engage him in conversation—urgently, awkwardly warm on their side, full of self-conscious laughter; and on his side, studiously attentive but maddeningly noncommittal. People talked about the fact that he went every week to dine at the Abernathy home, whether Tom was there or not. They noticed when Susan took him to the barber shop and when they drove together to La Crosse to visit the mall. Her good humor began to irritate the other women in ways it never had before, and their eyes followed her when she passed by.

"She must of kissed that frog good, 'cause he sure turned into a prince," said Jewell Hogan at the beauty salon, and the remark was considered so witty it was repeated all over town.

For herself, Susan had found one more reason to love her life in Okanoggan Falls just before losing it. She was playing a game that gave her life an exotic twist, excitement it had lacked. It was her patriotic duty to lie awake each morning, thinking of ways to get closer to a thrillingly attractive, powerful man who clearly enjoyed her company and relied on her in some unusually intimate ways. Her own success astonished her. In the last month before it was scheduled to fall apart, her life had become nearly perfect.

Between arranging to move his business and the mayoral duties, Tom was often gone on the nights when Captain Groton came over for dinner. Susan was aware of the gossip—a blushing Nick had told her the boys were taunting him about his mother—but she was not about to let small-mindedness stop her. "Just wait till they see how it pays off," she said to Nick.

It made her think she needed to start making it pay off.

By now, Captain Groton was perforce conversant with the ceremonial foods of the Midwest—string-bean casserole, jello salad, brats and beans—and the communal rituals at which they were consumed. So Susan had been entertaining herself by introducing him to more adventurous cuisine. His tastes were far less conservative than Tom's, and he almost invariably praised her efforts. On one night when Tom was returning late, she ordered a pizza for the boys and prepared shrimp with wild rice, cilantro, artichokes, and sour cream, with just a hint of cayenne pepper and lemon. They ate in the dining room with more wine than usual.

The captain was telling her how the amateur scholar who ran the landfill, in one of the endless efforts to deter the Wattesoons from their plans, had tried to convince him that there was an important archaeological site with buried treasure underneath the town. He had even produced proof in the form of an old French map and a photo of a metallic object with a mysterious engraved design.

Susan laughed, a little giddy from the wine. "You didn't fall for it, did you?"

Captain Groton looked at her quizzically. "No, I didn't fall down."

His English was so good she almost never encountered a phrase he didn't know. "It's an expression, to fall for something. It means he was pulling your leg."

"Pulling my leg. And so I was supposed to fall down?"

"No, no," she said. "It's just an idiom. To fall for something is to be deceived. On the other hand, to fall for some*one* means to become fond of them, to fall in love."

He considered this thoughtfully. "You use the same expression for being deceived and falling in love?"

It had never struck her before. "I guess we do. Maybe it means that you have to have illusions to fall in love. There *is* a lot of self-deception involved. But a lot of truth as well."

She suddenly became aware how seriously he was watching her, as if the topic had been much on his mind. When their eyes met, she felt a moment of spontaneous chemical reaction; then he looked away. "And when you say 'Okanoggan Falls,' which do you mean, deception or love?" he asked.

"Oh, love, no question."

"But if it meant deception, you would not tell me," he said with a slight smile.

"I am not deceiving you, captain," she said softly. And, a little to her own surprise, she was telling the truth.

There was a moment of silence. Then Susan rose from the table, throwing her napkin down. "Let's go to the back yard," she said.

He followed her out into the hot summer night. It was late August; the surrounding yards were quiet except for the cicadas buzzing in the trees and the meditative sigh of air conditioners. When they reached the deeper grass under the trees, the captain came to a halt, breathing in the fragrant air.

"The thing I was not expecting about being human is the skin," he said. "It is so sensitive, so awake."

"So you like it now, being human?" she asked.

"There are compensations," he said, watching her steadily.

Her intellect told her she ought to be changing the subject, pressing him on the topic of public concern, but her private concerns were flooding her mind, making it impossible to think. She was slightly drunk, or she never would have said it aloud. "Damn! It's so unfair. Why does such a perfect man have to be an alien?"

A human man would have taken it as an invitation. Captain Groton hesitated, then with great restraint took her hands chastely in his. "Susan," he said, "There is something I need to explain, or I would be deceiving you." He drew a breath to steady himself as she watched, puzzled at his self-consciousness. He went on, "It is not an accident, this shape I have assumed. On my planet, when a woman chooses a man, he becomes what she most wishes him to be. It is the function of the chameleon trait. We would have died out long ago without it." He gave a slight smile. "I suppose nature realized that men can never be what women really want until they are created by women."

Susan was struggling to take it in. "Created by…? But who created you?"

"You did," he said.

"You mean—"

"That first day we met, when you touched me. It is why we avoid human contact. A touch by the right woman is enough to set off the reaction. After that, physiology takes over. Every time you touched me after that, it was biochemical feedback to perfect the process."

All the misery and shock of an interspecies transformation, and she had done it to him? "Oh my God, you must hate me," she said.

"No. Not at all."

Of course not. Her perfect man would never hate her. It would defeat the purpose.

At that thought, she felt like a bird that had flown into a window pane. "You mean you are everything I want in a man?" she said.

"Evidently."

"I thought Tom was what I wanted," she said faintly.

"You already have him," Captain Groton said. "You don't need another."

She studied his face, custom-made for her, like a revelation of her own psyche. It was not a perfect face, not at all movie-star handsome, but worn with the traces of experience and sadness.

"What about your personality?" she asked. "Did I create that, too?"

He shook his head. "That is all mine."

"But that's the best part," she said.

She couldn't see his face in the dim light, but his voice sounded deeply touched. "Thank you."

They were acting like teenagers. They *were* like teenagers, in the power of an unfamiliar hormonal rush, an evolutionary imperative. The instant she realized it, it shocked her. She had never intended to cheat on Tom, not for a nanosecond. And yet, it was as if she already had, in her heart. She had fantasized a lover into being without even realizing it. He was the living proof of her infidelity of mind.

Trying to be adult, she said, "This is very awkward, captain. What are we going to do?"

"I don't know," he said. "Perhaps—"

Just then, the back porch light came on, and they jumped apart guiltily, as if caught doing what they were both trying to avoid thinking about.

Tom was standing on the back porch, looking out at them. "You're back!" Susan called brightly, hoping her voice didn't sound as strained as she felt. She started up the lawn toward the house, leaving Captain Groton to follow. "Have you eaten?"

"Yes," Tom said. "I stopped at the Burger King in Walker."

"Oh, poor dear. I was just about to make coffee. Want some?"

"I am afraid I must be getting back to base," Captain Groton said.

"Won't you even stay for coffee?" Susan said.

"No, it is later than I realized." With a rueful laugh he added, "Now I understand why humans are always late."

She went with him to the front door, leaving Tom in the kitchen. The captain hesitated on the steps. "Thank you, Susan," he said, and she knew it wasn't for dinner.

Softly, she said, "Your women are lucky, captain."

Seriously, he said, "No, they're not."

"Their lives may be brief, but I'll bet they're happy."

"I hope you are right." He left, hurrying as if to escape his memories.

When Susan went back into the kitchen, Tom said with studied casualness, "Did you make any headway with him?"

"No," she said. "He's very dutiful." She busied herself pouring coffee. When she handed him his cup, for the first time in their marriage she saw a trace of worry in his eyes. She set the cup down and put her arms around him. "Tom," she said fiercely, "I love you so much."

He said nothing, but held her desperately tight.

And yet, that night as she lay awake listening to Tom's familiar breathing, questions crowded her mind.

There was a hole in her life she had not even known was there. Now that she knew it, she could not ignore the ache. She had settled into a life of compromises, a life of good-enough. And it was no longer good enough.

Yet there was no way for her to have more without hurting Tom. She didn't love him any less for the revelation that he wasn't perfect for her; he was human, after all. None of this was his fault.

She looked at the lump of covers that was her husband and thought of all she owed him for years of loyalty and trust. Somehow, she needed to turn from possibility and desire and pass on by. She had to reconcile herself to what she had. It was simply her duty.

The day of the move was planned down to the last detail, the way the Wattesoons did everything. Fleets of moving vans, hired from all over the region, would descend on Okanoggan Falls starting at 6:30 AM. After stopping at the Wattesoon base, they would roll into town at 8:00 sharp and fan out to assigned locations. The schedule of times when each household would be moved had been published in the paper, posted in the stores, and hand-delivered to each doorstep. There was a web site where everyone could find their own move time.

The protesters were organized as well. The word had gone out that everyone was to gather at 7:00 AM in the park opposite Town Hall. From there, they would march down Main Street to the spot where the highway ran between the bluff and the river, and block the route the trucks would have to take into town.

When Susan and Tom pulled into the mayor's reserved parking spot behind Town Hall at 6:45, it was clear the rally had drawn a crowd. The local police were directing traffic and enforcing parking rules, but not otherwise interfering. Lines of people carrying homemade signs, thermos bottles, and lawn chairs snaked toward the park, as if it were a holiday. Some activists Susan didn't recognize were trying to get a hand-held PA system going.

When Tom and Susan reached the front steps of Town Hall, Walt Nodaway, the Police Chief, saw them and came up. "We've got some professionals from out of town," he said. "Probably drove in from Madison."

"You have enough guys?" Tom asked.

"As long as everyone stays peaceable."

"The officers know not to interfere?"

"Oh, yeah." They had talked it over at length the night before.

A reporter came up, someone from out of town. "Mayor Abernathy, are you here to support the protesters?" she asked.

Tom said, "Everyone has a right to express their opinions. I support their right whether I agree with them or not."

"But do you agree with the people resisting the relocation?"

Susan had coached him not to say "No comment," but she could tell he wanted to right now. "It's hard on people. They want to defend their homes. I know how they feel." Susan squeezed his hand to encourage him.

The city council members had begun to arrive, and they gathered on the steps around Tom, exchanging low-toned conversations and watching the crowd mill around. The protest was predictably late getting started; it was 7:30 before the loudspeaker shrieked to life and someone started to lead a chorus of "We Shall Not Be Moved." People were starting to line up for the two-block march down to the highway when, from the opposite direction, a familiar black SUV came speeding around the police barricades and pulled up in front of Town Hall. A van that had been following it stopped on the edge of the park.

Captain Groton got out, followed by three Wattesoon guards who looked even more lumpish than usual beside their lean commander. All were in sand-colored uniforms. The captain cast an eye over the park, where people had just started to realize that the opposition had arrived, and then he turned to mount the steps. When he came up to Tom he said in a low, commanding voice, "A word with you, Mayor Abernathy. Inside." He turned to the city council members. "You too." Then he continued up the steps to the door. The others followed.

A few spectators were able to crowd inside before the Wattesoon guards closed the doors; Susan was one of them. She stood with the other onlookers at the back of the room as Captain Groton turned to the city officials.

They had never seen him really angry before, and it was an unsettling sight. There was a cold intensity about him, a control pulled tight and singing. "I am obliged to hold all of you responsible for the behavior of those people outside," he said. "They must return to their homes immediately and not interfere with the operation in progress." He turned to Tom. "I would prefer that the order come from you, Mayor."

"I can't give them that order," Tom said. "For one, I don't agree with it. For two, they're not going to obey it, regardless of what I say. I'm not their commander, just their mayor. They elected me, they can un-elect me."

"You have a police force at your disposal."

"Just Walt and three officers. They can't act against the whole town. There must be four hundred people out there."

"Well then, consider this," Captain Groton said. "I *do* have a force at my disposal. Two hundred armed soldiers. Ten minutes ago, they started to surround the park outside. They are only waiting for my order to move in and start arresting non-compliants. We have a secure facility ready to receive prisoners. It is your decision, Mayor."

They had not expected such heavy-handed tactics. "There are children out there, and old people," Tom protested. "You can't have soldiers rough them up. They're just expressing their views."

"They have had three months to express their views. The time for that is over."

"The time for that is never over," Tom said.

Their eyes met for a moment, clashing; then Captain Groton changed his tone. "I am at my wit's end," he said. "You have known from the beginning what we were here for. I have never lied to you or concealed anything. I have done everything in my power to make you content. I have compromised till my superiors are questioning my judgment. And still you defy me."

"It's not you, captain," Tom said in a more conciliatory tone. "You've been very fair, and we're grateful. But this is about something bigger. It's about justice."

"Justice!" Captain Groton gave a helpless gesture. "It is about fantasy, then. Something that never was, and never will be. Tell me this: do you call the earthquake unjust, or march against the storm?"

"Earthquakes and storms aren't responsible for their actions. They don't have hearts, or consciences."

"Well, if it would help reconcile you, assume that we don't, either."

With a level gaze, Tom said, "I know that's not true."

For a moment Captain Groton paused, as if Tom had scored a hit. But then his face hardened. "I have misled you, then," he said. "We are implacable as a force of nature. Neutral and inevitable. Neither your wishes, nor mine, nor all those people's out there can have the slightest influence on the outcome."

Outside, the crowd had gathered around the steps, and now they were chanting, "The people, united, will never be defeated." For a moment the sound of their voices was the only thing in the room.

In a low tone, Captain Groton said, "Show some leadership, Tom. Warn them to get out of here and save themselves. I can give you ten minutes to persuade them, then I have to give the order. I'm sorry, but it is my duty."

Tom stared at him, furious to be made into a collaborator. Captain Groton met his gaze levelly, unyielding. Then, for an instant, Tom glanced at Susan. It was very quick, almost involuntary, but everyone in the room saw it. And they knew this was about more than principle.

Tom drew himself up to his full height, his spine visibly stiffening. Ordinarily, he would have consulted with the council; but this time he just turned and walked to the door. As he passed by, Susan fell in at his side. The onlookers made way. Not a soul knew what Tom was going to do.

Outside, the Wattesoon guards keeping the crowd away from the door fell back when Tom came out onto the steps. He held up his hands and the chanting faltered to a stop. "Listen up, everyone," he started, but his voice didn't carry. He gestured at the woman with the portable loudspeaker, and she hurried up the steps to give him the microphone.

"Listen up, everyone," he said again. The crowd had fallen utterly silent, for they saw how grim his face looked. "The Wattesoon soldiers have surrounded us, and in ten minutes they're going to move in and start arresting people."

There was a stir of protest and alarm through the crowd. "They're bluffing," someone called out.

"No they're not," Tom said. "I know this captain pretty well by now. He's dead serious. Now, if you want to get arrested, roughed up, and put in a Wattesoon jail, fine. But everyone else, please go home. Take your kids and get out of here. I don't want you to get hurt. You know they can do it."

On the edges, some people were already starting to leave; but most of the crowd still stood, watching Tom in disappointment, as if they had expected something different from him. "Look, we did our best," he said. "We talked them into a lot of things I never thought they'd give us. We pushed it as far as we could. But now we've reached the point where they're not going to give any more. It's our turn to give in now. There's nothing more we can do. Please, just go home. That's what I'm going to do."

He handed the mike back to its owner and started down the steps. Susan took his hand and walked with him. There was a kind of exhalation of purpose, a deflation, around them as the crowd started breaking up. Though one of the protesters from Madison tried to get things going again, the momentum was gone. People didn't talk much, or even look at each other, as they started to scatter.

Halfway across the park, Susan whispered to Tom, "The car's the other way."

"I know," Tom said. "I'll come back and get it later." She figured out his thinking then: the symbolic sight of them walking away toward home was the important thing right now.

Don't look back, she told herself. It would make her look hesitant, regretful. And yet, she wanted to.

When they reached the edge of the park, she couldn't help it, and glanced over her shoulder. The green space was almost empty, except for a little knot of diehards marching toward the highway to block the trucks. On the steps of Town Hall, Captain Groton was standing alone. But he wasn't surveying the scene or the remaining protesters. He was looking after her. At the sight, Susan's thoughts fled before a breathtaking rush of regret, and she nearly stumbled.

"What is it?" Tom said.

"Nothing," she answered. "It's okay."

By evening of the second day, it was all over in Okanoggan Falls.

In Red Bluff, there had been an insurrection; the Wattesoon army was still fighting a pitched house-to-house battle with resisters. In Walker, the soldiers had herded unruly inhabitants into overcrowded pens, and there had finally been a riot; the casualty reports were still growing. Only in Okanoggan Falls had things gone smoothly and peacefully.

The moving van had just pulled away from the Abernathy home with Tom and Nick following in the pickup, and Susan was making one last trip through the house to spot left-behind items, when her cell phone rang. Assuming it was Tom, she didn't look at the number before answering.

"Susan."

She had not expected to hear his voice again. All the decisions had been made; the story was over. The Wattesoons had won. Okanoggan had fallen to its enemies.

"Can you spare five minutes to meet me?" he said.

She started to say no, but the tug of disappointment made her realize there was still a bond between them. "Not here," she said.

"Where?"

"On Main Street."

Ben was in the back yard, taking an emotional leave of the only home he had known. Susan leaned out the back door and called, "I have to run into town for a second. I'll pick you up in ten minutes."

Downtown, the streetlights had come on automatically as evening approached, giving a melancholy air to the empty street. The storefronts were empty, with signs saying things like "Closed For Good (or Bad)" tacked up in the windows. As Susan parked the car, the only other living things on Main Street were a crow scavenging for garbage and Captain Groton, now sole commander of a ghost town.

At first they did not speak. Side by side, they walked down the familiar street. Inside Meyer's Drugstore, the rack where Susan had bought him a magazine was empty. They came to the spot where they had watched the Fourth of July parade, and Captain Groton reached out to touch the warm brick.

"I will never forget the people," he said. "Perhaps I was deceiving myself, but in the end I began to feel at ease among them. As if, given enough time, I might have been happy here."

"It didn't stop you from destroying it," Susan said.

"No. I am used to destroying things I love."

If there had been self-pity in his voice she would have gotten angry; but it was simply a statement.

"Where will you go next?" she asked.

He hesitated. "I need to clear up some disputes related to this assignment."

Behind them a car door slammed, and Captain Groton cast a tense look over his shoulder. Following his gaze, Susan saw that a Wattesoon in a black uniform had emerged from a parked military vehicle and stood beside it, arms crossed, staring at them.

"Your chauffeur seems to be impatient."

"He is not my chauffeur. He is my guard. I have been placed under arrest."

Susan was dumbstruck. "What for?"

He gave a dismissive gesture. "My superiors were dissatisfied with my strategy for completing my assignment."

Somehow, she guessed it was not the use of force he meant. "You mean…" She gestured at his human body.

"Yes. They felt they needed to take a stand and refer the matter to a court martial."

Susan realized that this was what he had wanted to tell her. "But you succeeded!" she said.

He gave an ironic smile. "You might argue that. But a larger principle is at stake. They feel we cannot risk becoming those we conquer. It has happened over and over in our history."

"It happens to us, too, in our way," Susan said. "I think your officers are fighting a universal law of conquest."

"Nevertheless, they look ahead and imagine Wattesoon children playing in the schoolyards of towns like this, indistinguishable from the humans."

Susan could picture it, too. "And would that be bad?"

"Not to me," he said.

"Or to me."

The guard had finally lost his patience and started toward them. Susan took the captain's hand tight in hers. "I'm so sorry you will be punished for violating this taboo."

"I knew I was risking it all along," he said, gripping her hand hard. "But still…" His voice held a remarkable mix of Wattesoon resolution and human indignation. "It is unjust."

It was then she knew that, despite appearances, she had won.

The Conservator

A conservator is a scientist whose job is to freeze time. Her tools are chemistry, the microscope, and the exotic ends of the spectrum. She analyzes the composition of materials and their molecular interactions with air, humidity, and each other in order to prevent decay. Oxidation, acidification, light, and microbial life are her opponents; the inert and dark are her servants. The touch of her brush or scalpel can bring eternal youth, but not to you or me—only to unliving things.

She does not choose the things to which she grants immortality. That decision is made by other gods—wealthy donors, granting agencies, The Market. Not everything can be saved: only those objects that define who we are better than we are able to do ourselves.

The Archive that had contracted for the Conservator's services was housed in a domed stone building on the edge of a park. Two flights of stairs, split apart like encircling arms, led up to the tall bronze doors. Above the entry, dark windows arched their eyebrows down at anyone climbing the steps. The building had once been a synagogue, but its congregation abandoned it, moving west. Rescued and readapted, all its sacred symbols expunged, it became a temple for preservation of the past.

The Conservator arrived at 5:00, closing time. It was already dark, and a drizzle was falling, making the pavement reflect the streetlights. The Conservator mounted the steps, a tall figure in her dark raincoat, the hood drawn up to cover her unkempt gray hair, her long, bony hands thrust into the pockets. The Archivist met her at the door and locked it behind her. "Thank you for coming at this hour. We don't have any space large enough for this, except the reading room. We had to wait until the researchers were gone."

The Archivist was well preserved herself. She had been a pretty woman, once, with a china-doll complexion. Her face was still flawless, almost frozen into an expression that conveyed unshakable confidence within her domain. She moved with a precise, controlled economy. In a field around her, everything was in place. The sight of such perfect skin made the Conservator feel cadaverous. Time had not treated her so kindly.

Together, they passed through the lobby into the reading room. It had been the main sanctuary of the temple. Above them hung a lofty dome, ornate with gilded plasterwork. At its apex, a discreet drape hid the Star of David. On the broad circle of terrazzo floor, two maintenance men and two young assistant archivists were busy moving the library tables to the edge of the room, clearing a space in the middle.

"It is so difficult to get this document out, we almost never do it," the Archivist said, making conversation. "It's kept in a storeroom underneath there, where the altar used to be."

"How did you acquire it?" the Conservator asked. Provenance was sometimes useful to know.

"It has always been here. It was part of the original collection."

The archivists were spreading a dropcloth, so the Conservator went to check her equipment, delivered yesterday and stacked along the wall in the shadows behind the aged card catalog. One of the maintenance men came over to help her string extension cords for the lights on tripod stands.

"Are you ready for us to bring it out?"

"Whenever you like," the Conservator said.

The lights came on, creating a cocoon of artificial brightness under the darkened dome. The two assistant archivists held open the double doors, and the maintenance men maneuvered through with an enormous muslin-wrapped roll on their shoulders. Obeying the Archivist's precise instructions, they brought it to the center of the room and laid it on the dropcloth. The assistants knelt down to untie the fabric laces that secured the covering.

The Conservator drew close as they began to unroll the document. It had been described to her, but it was more compelling in reality. Her mind sharpened with a cold rush of vitality. She was in the presence of the thing to which she was most devoted: the authentic artifact, the tangible object on whose surface the past was written in cypher.

It was a map of the great river, source to mouth, drawn in uncanny detail. And yet, as it unrolled before her, the Conservator could see it was no ordinary map. Six feet wide and thirty long, it was a layered creation, many-leaved as fillo dough. She drew on latex gloves and knelt to finger its edge. Not only were there layers, but they were of different materials, bonded securely together. The bottom layer was a milky-white cured hide, soft and supple. Then there was a sheet of thin, pliable birchbark taken from the inner layer of the tree, once colored a pinkish beige but now browned with time. Then a layer of parchment followed by one of laid paper—the hand-crafted kind that still showed the ladderlike pattern of the screen on which it was made. Next was a layer of higher-quality wove paper, and one of the sized linen once used for architectural drawings. The topmost layer was a brittle, yellowed paper, disintegrating in snowflake bits that already littered the dropcloth.

"It's ironic that the most recent layer is in the worst shape," the Archivist said. She sounded tragic, not ironic.

"Not unusual, though," the Conservator said. It was wood-pulp paper, a mass manufacturing process introduced in the 1880s that resulted in such a high acid content that the material literally self-destructed. In all the archives of the country, the recent paper was eating itself away even when stored in perfect conditions. Inherent vice, conservators called it. Most of the printed history of the twentieth century would be gone before another hundred years passed. It was inscribed on an evanescent surface.

The Conservator stood pondering the problem. Any composite document was a challenge, since what cures one substance destroys another. Paper could be deacidified by soaking in distilled water, but that would damage the other layers. "Do you know what is on the layers underneath?" she asked.

The Archivist gestured. "Only what we can see."

The top layer appeared to be a Corps of Engineers map of the gigantic hydrological project that transformed the river in the twentieth century, when the government collared the tumultuous brown giant with a chain of dams, dredgings, and riprap. Instead of a free-flowing, natural river, it had become a series of slowly seeping pools, kept to an artificial year-round nine-foot channel for the passage of barges. Despite its crumbling condition, the map still exuded the confidence of the great twentieth-century public-works project. It celebrated victory over primordial forces.

In the places where the paper had flaked away, the layer underneath showed through. It was the one on linen and appeared to be a navigational chart used by river boats in the years before the damming and dredging. Shoals and bayous emerged from under the engineered river, chaotic meanderings and hazards long erased from the land.

There was a place where the linen also had worn thin, and the Conservator gestured the archivists to switch off the floodlights while she took her hand-held UV light and held lit the surface with it. A ghost of the ink underneath showed through. It appeared to be a plat map made by the government surveyors who first divided up the continent into a neat gridwork of townships, ranges, and sections for sale to incoming settlers. The geometric pattern ran right up to the edge of the river, then surrendered to the complex braidwork of channels, the half-land, half-water—impossible to own or encompass in a net of longitude.

Below that, even the UV could not penetrate. But that was why the Conservator had brought her arsenal of equipment.

It took a long time to set up the framework that supported the imaging device, a web of metal struts built over the document, with the lights and camera assembly riding on metal rails, pointing down. The cables from the camera ran into the Conservator's computer. At last, images started to flow along the wires, showing the document in every wavelength from infrared to X-ray. The camera whirred steadily down the rails, pausing every few feet. The archivists went to the staff lounge for a cup of coffee, since it would be a long time before the composite image was complete.

The Conservator sat alone before the phosphorescent screen. Around her, the dome was dark and silent except for the drip, drip of a leak somewhere. She monitored the quality of the images, trying different settings to achieve the best resolution. The bottom layers were the most difficult to capture. Slightly altered settings gave puzzlingly different results.

Even before the camera had finished its slow journey up the river, the Conservator had guessed the results of her electromagnetic archaeology. The fourth layer, the one on laid paper, appeared to be an early military map, perhaps made when the river was a boundary between contested European empires. It charted potential fortification sites where the passage of invading armies could be controlled.

The fifth layer had captions written in a crabbed hand in Latin. From the devotional names given to various tributaries, this cartographer seemed to be a missionary, perhaps a Recollect or Jesuit, intent on inscribing the names of Christian saints and symbols onto the river he had discovered for the glory of God.

The sixth and seventh layers were altogether different. The one on birchbark was a linear diagram: a long chain of rectangles and cartouches populated by a hallucinatory set of creatures. There were horned panthers guarding the gates at certain points, and clusters of figures with human heads but bodies like tombstones. There were bears with lines running down their throats to their hearts, and triangular birds with lightning darting from their eyes.

The Archivist arrived back as the Conservator was studying an image of layer six. "Have you ever seen anything like this?" the Conservator asked.

"I think we have a book that shows something similar," the Archivist replied. She crossed to the card catalog to look up a call number, then sent one of the assistants down to the stacks to fetch it.

It was a book about the sacred birchbark scrolls of the original Algonquian inhabitants of the upper river. The illustrations showed what looked like partial renditions of the master diagram before them. The Archivist skimmed some pages, then read aloud:

The scrolls portray both a historical and symbolic landscape. The journey they chart is the migration of the tribe from its ancestral homeland, but also that of an individual soul from ignorance to enlightenment. The scrolls map the challenges faced by the tribe in their immemorial exodus up the river and the dangers that confront the individual who seeks to travel the *Mdewiwin* way. At each step, the initiate must confront the spirit beings who symbolize flaws in his or her own soul and pass through death and rebirth into a new stage of life, aided by the redeeming power of the *megis*. The scrolls may justly be compared to the Egyptian Book of the Dead as a guide through moral dangers to a promised land; but the Algonquian guide is a Book of Life.

"Is there a dotted line?" the Archivist asked, peering at the screen.

"Yes, here," the Conservator said, tracing it with her finger.

"That shows the route the individual must follow."

It was a complex route, sometimes backtracking, sometimes moving in a spiral. In some places, it skirted the animal shapes in its path, and sometimes it confronted and passed between them. It was difficult for the Conservator to imagine how anyone could make the proper choices without the map.

As they were studying layer six, the camera finished its survey and shut down. The Conservator had been waiting for this to study the lowest layer, since it was an image that had to be seen whole.

When she called it up on the screen, it was as she had surmised: the painting of a stylized snake, rendered in black and red on the white surface of the hide.

Outside the dome, there was a flash of lightning, and the crack of thunder came almost immediately after. For an instant the lights dimmed, but the computer stayed on. They could hear the barrage of rain far above them.

On either side of the snake was a half-circle of feathers with red stems and black tips, fanned out in a sunburst shape.

The Conservator looked up at the Archivist. With her face harshly lit by the screen, the Archivist looked more wrinkled and pasty, as if she had suddenly aged. "A feathered serpent?" the Conservator asked. "Is that part of North American mythology?"

"I don't know," said the Archivist. "Let me look it up."

While the Archivist was doing that, the Conservator took notes on damage and deterioration. The bottom edge of the document was frayed and stained, as if it had been dragged through mud, obscuring the mouth of the river. In the middle layers, there was one bad tear slashing diagonally right across the river. One of the young assistant archivists, looking over her shoulder, said, "Interesting place for a rip."

"What do you mean?"

He pointed. "That's Reelfoot Lake, and there is New Madrid. Site of the worst earthquake ever recorded in North America, in 1811. They say it made church bells ring in Philadelphia. At first the river flowed backwards, then cut a whole new channel. The rip is right at the New Madrid fault."

"Well, it seems to be stabilized now," the Conservator said. "The layers above it have prevented the tear from spreading."

There was other hidden damage: a set of old scorch marks across the northern forests at the top end, signs of old insect infestation on layer three, water damage so bad in places that the inked edges of the river had become indistinct. The Conservator mapped it all, square by square.

The Archivist returned with a book about painted skin robes. One photograph showed a robe with a snake running down its length. "The caption says it disappeared from a museum in Paris in 1982, presumed stolen," she said.

"What does the snake mean?"

She browsed the text, then said, "They think the Paris robe was a copy of one from a sacred bundle that could only be viewed during the summer, at a ceremony celebrating the origins of the tribe. It is a mnemonic diagram symbolizing the story of how the people emerged from an underground country near the snake's tail, and for centuries traveled up the snake's back. The snake represents both the river and time. Events become more recent farther up the snake, and the future is near its head. On other robes, the snake is shown coiled in a spiral, because time was regarded as both linear and cyclical."

"So the river is a snake, and the snake is time," the Conservator mused. In her world, things could not be two things simultaneously. Nothing could be both dermis and lignin, both oak gall and ochre. But this document was clearly an exception.

Part of the scan on her screen was of lower quality than the rest, so the Conservator punched in the coordinates to send the camera back for a second scan while she took a tiny sample of each layer with a tweezer, to study at her lab with microscope and mass spectrometer. She put them in plastic bags the size of digital camera chips. One of the assistant archivists came in from the lobby, where he had been staring out the door. “You should see it coming down out there,” he said. “The water is up over the street curbs.” No one answered.

The new image, when it appeared on the screen, was of higher quality, but something about it made the Conservator click back to the original scan so she could compare them. Sure enough, one of the curves of the snake had shifted slightly between the two scans. She checked to make sure she had not typed in the wrong coordinates. There was no mistake. The Archivist, looking over her shoulder, had an anxious expression.

“We’ve had the same problem, trying to photograph it,” she said in a low tone, as if afraid someone might hear. “It’s as if the document distorts like rubber. Sometimes the ink seems to flow. We need to stabilize it. Isn’t there anything you can do?”

Thoughtfully, the Conservator said, “Of course there is. We could encase it in a nitrogen atmosphere, freeze it in time. It would be very expensive. Is that what you want?”

"Yes!" the Archivist said. "I don't care what it costs. We need to stop it from changing." She sounded a little desperate. "That is why archives exist, to save things."

"It's not always good to prevent things from changing," the Conservator said softly. "Especially rivers. They meander, erode, fight back."

"I don't want any erosion. Not in my archive. It is not your job to question us. We hired you to come up with a solution."

"All right." The Conservator began to shut down her equipment. "I have all the information I need. I will study it and send you my proposal."

It took much less time to break down the equipment than it took to set it up. The archivists all helped, as if in a hurry to roll up the map and store it away again. Soon the men carried it off on their shoulders, leaving only a snowfall of brittle paper particles on the carpet to show it had been there.

"Be careful outside," the Archivist warned as the Conservator shrugged on her raincoat. "There are flash flood warnings." The Archivist seemed a little embarrassed now about her previous unseemly vehemence.

"I'll be in touch," the Conservator promised.

It was past midnight, but the Conservator felt no desire for sleep. Outside, the rain was now falling gently, and the water had begun to recede, leaving a litter of leaves and gravel where it rose over the lawn. Her rental car had a water line on the side, but it started without trouble.

She was staying in a hotel downtown, by the river, but she did not go there at once. Instead, she drove until she found a steep, brick-paved street that ran down to the riverbank and parked the car. It was very late, very deserted. To her left towered the piers of an old stone and iron bridge; ahead, the street narrowed to run through a gate in the massive concrete floodwall that protected the city. Walking toward the levee, the Conservator encountered a bronze historical marker that informed her she was looking at the first railroad bridge to span the river, built 1874. It was an extraordinary engineering feat, for the river fought back fiercely. Fourteen men died building its footings.

She climbed a set of stone steps that led up to the bridge deck. At first she was puzzled by the lack of traffic. Then she saw that the span didn't lead much of anywhere any more: only to a derelict industrial district on the other side. No one was going there this time of night. The city had shifted, left the bridge behind, standing there gloriously obsolete.

Out over the river she walked, on the monumental shoulders of the ironwork arch. Below, the sinuous back of the river shimmered as with scales. Looking at it, she thought: What if this is the representation, and the other is the reality? It was not, she realized, a new thought. Uncounted generations of mankind had assumed that the landscape in which they lived was a symbol, a shadow-image of reality. The *new* thought was what propelled people to assemble the towers of the city, sink the piers of the bridge, erect the floodwalls along the banks: the thought that this is all there is.

And yet, the surface was crumbling away, eaten by its own acid. For two hundred years people had swarmed like tiny letters on a document, just to assemble a veneer over something they didn't believe in—an underlying blueprint we all must follow, a map of our route through time.

Leaning against the stone parapet, the Conservator gazed south, downstream, toward the past. There, the city lay gleaming. She wondered: Could I save all this from perishing? Could I stop the decay, freeze time, encapsulate it in an oxygen-free microclimate of inert materials? With my science, create a patch of earth immune from age and change?

She fingered the plastic bags in her pocket, containing the samples.

Pushing away from the railing, she crossed the empty bridge to look north, the direction of the future. Here, unlike the spangled southern view, the river was dark. Its turbid surface slid beneath her, flowing fast, too fast. It looked coiled, malicious, unsafe. A moment ago she had felt as if the power to dam it lay in her hands; now she felt overmatched.

The Conservator gazed off toward the source of time, wanting her eyes to adjust to this darkness, knowing they never would. Then she watched the plastic bags fall through her fingers and flutter down till they hit the surface of the water and were swept away.

About the Author

Carolyn Ives Gilman has been publishing science fiction and fantasy for almost twenty years. Her first novel, *Halfway Human,* published by Avon/Eos in 1998, was called "one of the most compelling explorations of gender and power in recent SF" by *Locus* magazine. Her short fiction has appeared in magazines and anthologies such as *Fantasy and Science Fiction, Bending the Landscape, The Year's Best Science Fiction, Realms of Fantasy, The Best From Fantasy & Science Fiction, Interzone, Universe, Full Spectrum,* and others. Her fiction has been translated into Italian, Russian, and German. In 1992 she was a finalist for the Nebula Award for her novella, "The Honeycrafters." Her novella *Candle in a Bottle* is also available from Aqueduct Press.

She is also a professional museologist and historian, specializing in North American history, particularly frontier and American Indian history. Her nonfiction books—as Carolyn Gilman—include *Where Two Worlds Meet: The Great Lakes Fur Trade* (1982), *The Way to Independence: Memories of a Hidatsa Indian Family, 1840-1920* (with Mary Jane Schneider), and *Lewis and Clark: Across the Divide.* She served as exhibition curator for the Missouri Historical Society's Lewis and Clark exhibition. She currently serves as senior exhibits developer at the National Museum of the American Indian in Washington, DC.

Made in the USA
Monee, IL
17 April 2026

48489183R00080